The Case of Eternal Blood

A Barry Hargrove Mystery

by Bob Nailor

I0518706

Copyright 2018 Bob Nailor
ISBN: 978-1-61877-164-3

Discover other titles by Bob Nailor
www.bobnailor.com

Table of Contents

Dedicated to

Denise Vitola

without whose mentoring over the years,
being an author would never have happened.
She persevered through my knuckle-headedness
to teach me the skills needed to write.
I'm glad to have you as a friend.

CHAPTER ONE

Total comfort. I sat in my office, feet up on the edge of the desk, trying to decide if I should go to lunch early, or finally start filing some of the paperwork stacked up in the corner. Glancing at the pile of ill-straightened file folders and assorted papers, suddenly, the lunch option was looking like a winner. Chinatown was only a couple of blocks away. Besides, I wasn't sure my stomach could handle the corner vendor, Juan's Tacos, and his barely cooked foods.

The phone rang.

Not one to hesitate, I snapped up the phone. "Hargrove Detective Agency."

"Hello?" The voice was timid, soft and immature-sounding.

"This is Barry Hargrove. May I help you?"

"How many times have I told you not..." CLICK.

I hung up the phone, all the while frowning at the woman's voice I'd heard in the background yelling at whoever had called, probably a kid by the sound. Obviously, lunch was definitely the proper choice of the hour. A quick shrug and a thumb to my nose with a wiggle of my fingers at the stack of papers, I flaunted I didn't need their approval. "Sorry, guys," I whispered with a total lack of sincerity and headed for the door with satisfaction filling my soul.

The phone rang, again. Two steps back and I had the receiver in hand once more. "Hargrove Detective Agency."

"Please help me," the young boy's voice pleaded. It was the young kid again. "My name is Marvin and—"

"Marvin! Put that..." CLICK.

Great! Some kid playing with the phone.

1

My mind raced with ideas of how to stop him from calling me. I looked down at the phone number, it was local. My first thought was to call the parents and have them address the issue with their son, but then I remembered his words: Help me.

The phone rang a third time. It was the same number. I picked up the receiver but before I could say anything...

"This is Marvin. Meet me at Chang's." CLICK.

That definitely had my interest. *Who is this Marvin person?* I thought him to be a child, but on this last call, the voice was mature and definitely in charge. Not to mention, Chang's wasn't the type of place where some kid could just wander in and take a seat.

I pressed the button on the answering machine and headed out the door, snapping the lock as I passed through the doorway to secure the office. Chang's was a great Chinese restaurant and a much better deal than Juan's Tacos. Street vendors usually had great fast food, and my iron stomach normally handled it well, but today, I just didn't want any of that. My mouth watered at the thought of sinking my teeth into some tasty authentic Mongolian food.

I dashed across the street, ambled down to the corner, turned and saw Chang's sign in the next block. My mind raced back to the phone call conversations. Marvin had called me three times. He needed help and wanted to meet me. I shook my head. I had no idea who I was meeting, or even what he looked like. Still, he seemed to know who I was. I shrugged. It was his call.

The great red, double doors with the matching golden dragons opened and I walked in. I surveyed the place. Things were pretty quiet at Chang's since it was still early for the lunch crowd. *Give it another fifteen minutes and this place will be bursting at the seams with customers vying for seats*, I thought and scanned the area. *Now where is –*

"Mr. Hargrove?" A man wearing heavy black-rimmed glasses sat two booths from the front door and motioned to me with his raised hand.

"Marvin?" I asked as I approached the booth, my hand extended. He didn't seem to want to shake, so I recovered by pretending to straighten the front of my jacket.

"Have a seat, Mr. Hargrove." He motioned me to the bench on the opposite side of the table. "I would like to apologize for this morning." Marvin glanced about the restaurant then stared down at the table while his fingers slowly shredded a corner of his paper napkin.

"You said you needed help — is that correct, Mr...?"

"I'm sorry. My name is Marvin Lan– uh, Marvin Lashlin." He stuck his hand out to shake.

"Detective Barry Hargrove, at your service." I shook his limp hand. "So how can I help you?"

Again, he gave a furtive look about the restaurant before he leaned in toward me conspiratorially. "A certain item has been stolen from my apartment."

"Nǐhǎo."

I glanced up to see Mei Lin standing there. She bowed her head to me. "You good, Mr. Hargrove?"

"I'm fine. Good to see you, Mei Lin," I replied. "Not sure what my friend would like, but does Chang have some his famous khorkhog ready today? I'm really craving Mongolian."

"Mr. Chang. No see him again today. I think he sick. No khorkhog three day now."

Marvin kept his profile low. "Vegetable lo mein... and water," he mumbled, never looking at our lovely waitress.

"Well, I'm hungry," I said. "Make it Orange Chicken on the spicy side, one egg roll and a pot of ginger tea." I smiled up at Mei Lin. "So Chang's sick? What do you think he has, Mei Lin?"

She shrugged, shook her head, bowed slightly then scurried off to get our orders.

I turned to Marvin. He was as white as baker's flour. "What's the problem?"

"Nothing," he snapped, yanked the glasses off and covered part of his face with his hand.

There was something going on as I could see him covertly peeking through his fingers at some point behind me. I turned to see who or what was causing Marvin's issues while pretending to be looking for Mei Lin. She turned and I raised my hand to get her attention, then stood and walked toward her while I searched the crowd at the doorway. All I saw was the typical group of people who clustered in every day from the surrounding offices. When I glanced back at the booth, Marvin had the luncheon menu up to cover his face.

"Yes?" Mei Lin asked.

"Could you bring two cups for the tea?"

She smiled politely, nodded before turning away from me. I took one last glimpse at the people near the door. The only ones who stood out to me were what seemed to be a husband and wife couple. They appeared to be very interested in the booth where Marvin was sitting. They stretched and gawked about the room, but they kept a close eye on Marvin's table. They turned and abruptly departed.

I slid into the booth and grabbed the menu from Marvin. "They're gone. Who were they? What did they want? Why were you scared." My machine gun attack of questions startled him.

He immediately dropped his eyes to the table, grabbed the napkin and again began to shred it.

"You either answer me or I tell Mei Lin my order is to go."

"She's my sister. They were looking for me since I left my apartment." He looked up at me and stared me eye-to-eye. "The last answer is simple. I'm not supposed to leave my apartment without them knowing." He bowed his head and mumbled, "I didn't tell them."

"Okay, fair enough. So you had something stolen. Did you notify the cops?"

"I can't notify them — that's why I called you."

"So what was stolen?"

The restaurant was filling, even more people stood at the door and the noise was unbelievable. At times I thought I'd have to yell for Marvin to hear me. While I watched him, he cringed as the mob continued to grow.

"Maybe we should have met at Juan's on the corner," I added with a smile. He didn't. Ignoring his sudden disdain, I pulled out my notepad to jot my notes.

4

"Somebody stole my e-reader."

"You're what?"

"My electronic reader," Marvin retorted and looked at my little wired notepad. "You know – My God, you don't have one?"

"I still prefer paper," I muttered realizing what he was referring to. "Give me a comfortable chair, a roaring fire, a fine cup of hot coffee and a book, the paper kind. That's how I roll, uh, er, read."

"I keep most of my work on the computer but—"

"Wait a minute," I yelled. "You have a computer and they steal your book reader? What the hell for, Marvin? You got some fancy porn or something on it?" I hadn't realized how loud my voice had become.

The restaurant was deadly quiet. I glared back at the people staring at us. Marvin cringed down into the booth.

Mei Lin maneuvered like a pro through the mob and slid up to the table with a tray of food. The din of other conversations once more filled the restaurant.

"Orange Chicken, Mr. Hargrove." Mei Lin placed the oval dish down and the heavenly scent of spicy orange filled my nostrils. "And your egg roll. Here is lo mein." She put that dish in front of Marvin. "Tea, two cups and one water." She smiled at us. "You want more?"

"We're fine, Mei Lin. Xièxie." She sauntered away to another table. I looked over at Marvin as he slurped up a noodle into his mouth. "Why would they take your reader and not your computer?"

"I'm sorry," Marvin whispered. "They took the stick drive and removable hard drive from the computer but those really aren't important items. I can live without them. I have almost all my stuff backed up and stored in a cloud elsewhere."

I nodded like I knew what this guy was talking about.

"But my reader; I store my important stuff on it." He trapped some noodles in his chopsticks and I watched as they slithered into his mouth with a resounding slurp. He chewed. "My diagrams and notes are concealed within the pages of a book." He looked furtively at me. "I need it back."

"Do you have any idea who stole it?" I popped a chicken

morsel covered with red chili flakes and rice into my mouth.

"It had to be somebody from the Ebersole Micro Intra-Techtonics Corporation, or perhaps hired by them."

"E-MIT-C? Why them?" His answer caught me off-guard and I choked on the swallow of spicy chicken.

"I worked..." He hesitated. "I worked for them before... before the... uh... before I got sick."

"Care to elaborate?" I manipulated the chopsticks, stuffed another tasty piece of rice-laden chicken into my mouth and chewed vigorously.

Marvin once more shrunk down into the booth. "I... It happened..." He hung his head.

"If you can't—" I started.

"Never mind," Marvin said and sat up with his head held high. "If you must know all the gory details then so be it." He looked down at his plate of lo mein. "Ugh. I loath this... this..." He made a grimace and then used the back of his hand to slide the platter off to the side. There was absolute disdain on his face. "Something with an essence of mild flavor such as found at Maison de Crêpes would have been much better than Chang's, but —" He wrinkled his nose, pursed his lips and slowly closed his eyes with a slight turn toward the inside of the establishment as if my appearance was also distasteful. "So, Detective Hargrove, you wish to know the reason for my leaving E-MIT-C. It's very simple. I had a breakdown. Seems the pressure of my work took its toll." He placed both hands on the table and folded them together in front of him and watched me.

I was caught off-guard by the sudden change in Marvin. One minute, a scared, mousy-type character and now he sat in front of me, totally in command.

"A nervous breakdown, eh?" I eyed him warily.

"I didn't say nervous, detective. Are you sure you're as good as you claim?"

"My apologies, Marvin. Exactly what type of breakdown did you have?"

Again, he turned and watched the other patrons, pursed his lips, and barely shook his head. I would have loved to been in his brain at that moment, seeing what he was thinking. He turned back to me and blinked, as if he had the rest of eternity to finish.

"It was P-T-S-D, post-traumatic stress disorder, if you must know. My work was sabotaged the day I was presenting it to the upper echelon of E-MIT-C."

"Sabotaged? By who?"

"Excuse me, detective, that is why I hired you. You are supposed to find out who did this to me. Who sabotaged my work? Who stole my reader, hard drive and..." He waved his hand in a dismissing manner. "...whatever else they took."

Right now I really didn't like Marvin. His arrogance was getting under my skin.

"Fine," I said. "My fee is one thousand a week to start plus all expenses." I figured he would freak at the cost.

"Is that all?" he sniveled. "Here." He reached into his pants pocket and withdrew a roll of bills which he plopped onto the table. "That is five grand. The quicker you resolve the issue, the more money you get to keep as a bonus." He sneered at me — I think it was supposed to be a smile. "I'd recommend you get working on this quickly." He glanced down at the remaining food on my plate. "May I suggest you take the rest of your meal with you in a to-go doggie bag?" He watched me. I didn't move. "Detective, remember tempus fugit." He raised a hand and snapped his fingers loudly. "Miss Mei Lin, our check."

My first reaction was total shock. I was being dismissed.

Mei Lin approached the table and frowned at Marvin. I had to agree with her; he was a totally different man as he snapped the bill from her fingers.

"Here," he said after a quick glance at the sheet of paper and grabbed three tens off the stack in front of me. "This will cover the cost of the meals and give you a tidy tip." He leaned forward, still holding tightly to the bills. "Miss Mei Lin, the next time I come into this establishment, please tell me how much I dislike Chinese food and don't let me in. Am I understood?"

She held onto the tens, frowned at his words and then looked at me, her eyes searching for an answer. I nodded my head.

"Y-y-yes sir," she whispered. "I tell you no come in."

He let go of the money and Mei Lin hustled away. Marvin stood then flipped a business card at me. "Here is the number you can reach me." He sauntered toward the door and disappeared.

I grabbed the card and stared at it.

Marvin Landelli, Sr. PhD
212-555-1937 X1003
E-MIT-C
NYC, NY

"Here is change, Mr. Hargrove." Mei Lin stood there with the bills and coins on a small tray.

"Keep it," I said. "He said it was the tip."

"You want dish to go?" She glanced at the plate of Orange Chicken.

Suddenly, I wasn't hungry anymore and shook my head. "Not this time, Mei Lin." I stood and wandered to the front door, pushing through the mob to breathe the fresh air outside.

He said his name was Marvin Lashlin. Who is this Landelli character? My mind raced to get answers, but none were forthcoming.

CHAPTER TWO

The spring air cleared my mind as I strolled back to my office, at least, I hoped it was clearing my mind. I continued to glance at Marvin's business card. The phone number was downtown. It hit me. This was his office number, but on the phone back in my office, I would have his home phone. It had to be since I'd heard a kid and woman. I picked up speed and waved at Juan on the corner. He smiled and proffered a taco, lifting it into the air at me. I waved him off with a loud 'Not today' and gave him a big smile.

I opened the door to the office, took one step inside. The phone rang.

"Hargrove Detective Agency."

"Be careful," the child's voice whispered then he giggled.

"Marvin! Put that pho–" CLICK.

I stood there listening to the dial tone, totally dumbfounded.

"Why would a small kid warn me?" I mumbled the words into the air for nobody in particular to hear. My mind strove to analyze what was going on, but it was like pushing through a huge pool of thick syrup. There had to an answer. I punched re-dial and waited.

The phone rang two times.

"Hello?"

I recognized that voice, it was Marvin Lashlin. "Ah, good, you're home," I said.

"Of course I'm home, Detective Hargrove. Where else would I be?"

"Yes, of course," I said apologetically. "I thought I would mention your son has been calling my –"

"My son? I don't have any children. I'm not married."

My knees buckled at his softly spoken words and I steadied myself up by locking my arm straight against my desk and slowly working my way around to the chair. I collapsed into it.

"Perhaps a nephew?" I offered.

"I live alone, Detective Hargrove." Suddenly his voice was firm, commanding. "Do you really have the time to be calling me and playing games?" He cleared his voice. "I suggest you begin your detective work elsewhere." He hung up.

Once more I listened to a dial tone buzz in my ear. I knew I'd heard a small boy's voice, and a woman's voice. One thing was for certain, I wasn't going crazy, at least, not yet.

The door opened and a couple strolled in, the male in the lead.

I stood. "May I help–" I recognized them immediately from the restaurant.

"Detective Hargrove," the man started and plopped in the chair on the opposite side of my desk. The woman stood behind him and placed her clasped hands on his shoulder. "We can dispense with the amenities." He gazed up at me with his dark blue eyes. "Please, sit down, detective." He motioned for me to take a seat. "You were contacted by a Marvin Lashlin." I sat, he leaned in, the woman's hands dropped off his shoulders. "I want you to drop the case immediately. It will be a waste of your time."

I leaned back in my chair, my hackles up just a bit. "Exactly why should I drop this case?" I had my pen in my fingers, manipulating it to keep me calm.

"Because Marvin doesn't have the money to pay you for your services," the woman said from behind the man. "I'm his sister. I know his finances. He's broke."

"I see," I said, which of course, I didn't see anything. I had a wad of bills in my pocket from Marvin which contradicted what these two were saying. None of this was making any sense. "What if I decided to do this ... uh, shall we say pro bono?"

The man leaned in closer, his elbow and arm on my desk. He narrowed his eyes as he looked at me. "Like I said, it will be a waste of your time. There is no case. Nothing was stolen. Marvin is a sick man."

"He didn't appear sick to me," I snapped back. The pen I'd been fiddling with slipped from my fingers onto the desk. It rolled across the desktop to just in front of the man. "Now, would you mind telling me exactly who you are? You come into my office with a lot of demands. What are your names?" I leaned forward, grabbed a sheet of paper and snatched the pen I'd fumbled just seconds earlier. I didn't know their names, but I knew who they were.

"My name is –" the woman started.

"He doesn't need any names," the man snarled at the woman. He stood, placed his fingertips on the desk, let them roll under his palms until only his knuckles were showing white as he leaned over the desk and glared at me. "Detective Hargrove is dropping this case. Isn't that right, detective?"

"Right now I'm on my way to the library, and then to the police precinct," I said with a smile while standing. "I'll take it under advisement. Until then..." I snapped my hand out to shake.

The man ignored me, turned, and headed out the door. The woman followed quickly behind him, her heels clicking loudly on the linoleum flooring.

I stood there watching them disappear behind the frosted glass of the door. I knew who they were the minute they walked in – they were Marvin's sister and her husband. Now I understood why Marvin had such a fear, not so much from his sister, but his brother-in-law was obviously another matter to be dealt with.

The library was a short trip and I fumbled around with the micro-fiche files, totally not understanding why the library continued to use it in our electronic world today. Still, I was able to read the issues of the newspaper where Dr. Marvin Landelli was scheduled to make his demonstration for the Ebersole Micro Intra-Techtronics Corporation. It was a mere month earlier. I found the article extremely interesting due to the fact Landelli was a bio-neurogenesist. I had no idea what that meant, but wrote it down for future reference. My two main concerns with regards to what I was reading was ... first: the conflict of work interests. E-MIT-C was a micro-computer based technology business. Landelli was a blood specialist, a hematologist extraordinaire. My mind spun at the concept of the two technologies working together. Yet, there was a lot medical technology being developed in the computer industry. Espionage was definitely something to consider. My second issue was names. I'd been tossed Lashlin when Marvin had first introduced himself and then it was Landelli. I was confused.

The picture came up. A revelation. It showed Landelli and five other people. The enlarger expanded the image and I hit the PRINT button. Along the bottom of the image were the names of the people in the picture: (l to r) James Harbinger, Marvin Landelli, Joyce Brenner, Timothy Ebersole & Jack Nusbaum. Four more people, two men and two women, milled in the background, but obviously, for purposes of the photo opportunity, weren't important. Two of the men were manipulating something which I hadn't noticed in the smaller image. It only became apparent when the picture was enlarged. Of the two women in the background, one had a questioning expression as she watched the two men. I scribbled into my notepad the four main names under the picture.

It seemed perhaps Marvin did have some facts to his tale and he had been sabotaged. It was photographed. I decided to print out the article since it was a very long article. I hoped maybe the four unknown people might be mentioned somewhere in the story.

I flipped my notepad closed, paid for my prints, and headed to the most logical person I knew who could help me. There was no doubt in my mind Sgt. Leroy Williamson would be thrilled to see me since I hadn't bothered him in a few weeks. After being partners for fifteen years before I struck out on my own to become a detective, he moved in another direction. I knew he worked Homicide and Missing Persons now, but the bottom line was simple – he was an inside contact for records, and I needed information on some people. Plus, with any luck, he might have some data on E-MIT-C and what was going on inside that big secret place.

###

The precinct hummed with activity as I wandered through the open room toward Williamson's desk. I nodded and smiled at a couple of people I recognized.

"I figured you'd come sniffing around shortly," Williamson muttered, giving me a side scowl as I walked up to his desk. Sweat beaded on his dark skin. He immediately ignored me and continued working on the paperwork he had in front of him. "It's been a while," he mumbled. "So whatever it is you're looking for, you ain't going to find it here. Just keep moving along, Hargrove." His two black index fingers punched the keys on his computer.

I flopped into the chair by his desk and smiled at him while putting an elbow on the desk, nudging some of his files out of the way. I made it obvious, I wasn't going away.

"Fine," Williamson snapped and grabbed the files and moved them to the other side of the desk. "I really don't have time today, Hargrove." He finally looked at me. "Why is it every time I get a case that is primo-sweet, you show up?"

"So what are you working on?" I asked innocently and stretched to look over at the file.

"Nothing you need to bother about," he said and closed the file folder, shoving the sheets in so I couldn't see them.

"Ah, Willie, you know I care about your work. C'mon, share."

Williamson leaned back in his chair and stared at me. I knew this wasn't good. He narrowed his eyes and then slowly blinked. "It really is none of your business, Hargrove. Need I state, police business? So what do you want?"

I was surprised by his curt manner, shrugged, and retrieved my notepad from my shirt pocket making sure the printout didn't accidentally fall out.

"Can you give me any information on these names?" I asked while offering the pad.

He took it and looked at the list. "Four? You have four missing people? How long?"

Without thinking I dropped my chin down and stared at my shoes. "They aren't missing." I heard my notepad drop on the desk near me.

"Ain't nothing I can do to help," Willie said. "Sorry." He carefully re-opened the file folder and deliberately covered the name so I couldn't read it.

"It's a case I'm working on," I whispered. "I was hired by a Marvin Lashlin or Landelli to find a stolen item — some sort of e-reader."

"Sorry, Barry, but I work on dead and missing people. People

13

have to be missing three days."

"Well, I was at Chang's today and—"

"You son-of-a-bitch!" Willie yelled, jumping out of his chair, knocking it over. My black friend towered over me. The precinct was dead silent. Williamson glanced about and then raised a hand to indicate things were okay. He reached down, set the chair back up then sat, leaned over and whispered, "How the hell did you read the name on this file?"

I reared back in my chair. "What you talking about?"

"Nothing." He slammed the file shut, opened a drawer and shoved it into the dark recesses, pushed the drawer closed then glared at me. "Give me your damned list." He grabbed the notepad I'd left on the desk.

"What was that all about?" I asked while standing since I knew Willie was going to the file cabinets.

"Sit your ass down, Hargrove," Willie snapped. "I will look this up on the computer." He glanced at me then gave me that grin only he can do. "So what is your case all about?" He turned to his computer and began typing on the keys.

"So that's how it works." I sat back down and leaned over the desk. "You won't tell me what you're working on, but expect me to spill my guts on my case."

"I'm not the guy looking for the information. So far, Marvin Landelli is clean, as is Marvin Lashlin." The fingers clicked on the keys. "Going to keep me in the dark?" The noise of the keys stopped. He paused, watching me out of the side of his eyes. "I'm waiting."

"Not sure of all the details, yet," I finally admitted. "I got a call, and went to Chang's for lunch. Met with this Marvin Lashlin guy and got paid five grand to locate a stolen item. I was handed a business card with Marvin Landelli's name on it. Then I get a visit from Lashlin's sister and heavy-handed brother-in-law who told me not to get involved." I sighed. "Let's see, a trip to the library, got these names, and well, now I'm here."

Willie started typing again. "I'm guessing you're taking the case?" The screen flashed. "Oh, this is interesting. Seems your guy Timothy Ebersole is popular with our fine staff. A high number of

14

speeding tickets, DUIs, parking tickets, a couple of accidents and one of my favorites, domestic violence involving a... lemme see... ah, yes, involving a Miss Joyce Brenner." He glanced down at the notepad. "And why... Lordy-be, she's next on the list." Willie turned to me. "You always bring the most interesting names to be checked."

"And you continually fight me every time, not wanting to help." I grinned back him. "Doesn't make sense, does it?" I nodded at the computer for him to continue.

"Miss Brenner only has the domestic violence and according to this, she called it in. Do you need more detail?"

I shook my head. "The fact it happened should be enough to get them to talk. What about the last two?"

"I'm working on it, *boss*."

I didn't miss the sneer.

"So, James Harbinger is clean and Jack Nusbaum has one DUI. So what is your next step?" Williamson turned and faced me.

"It's back to the office to allow all this to mull together and give me an answer." I reached over and grabbed my notepad. "You going to tell me what you're working on?"

"Nothing much. I got notified about a missing person early this morning and then Homicide hands me the body about two hours later."

"Homicide?"

"Seems my M.P. is dead. Now, you scoot so I can get back to real work. Remember, I'm employed here, you're not anymore." Williamson poised his two fingers above the keyboard. "You know, you can get a terminal installed for a small fee."

I stood, grinned, and shook Willie's hand. "But, I'd miss you and these wonderful chats."

Williamson made a face. "If you want any more free information, at least take me out to a meal. I feel so cheap."

"Tell you what," I said as I walked away. "Steaks on me. Friday. 7pm. How about Portofino's since I know the missus likes her lobster."

"You're on," Williamson replied. "My wife will love a night out. You're paying for the babysitter, too?" He started to snicker.

"Sure! Why not?" I turned back and yelled. "See you then."

I stumbled into Preston, knocking a few files to the floor.

"Hey, big detective guy, you gonna take me out, too?" he asked while puffing up his chest.

"You're not my type, Preston." I patted him on the shoulder. "My dates like champagne and look great in a slinky dress." I stood back. "You? Sorry, Pres, but you're just too frumpy." I made a face.

A loud round of jeers and laughter followed as I made for the exit, knowing full well Preston was fuming.

CHAPTER THREE

The office had warmed in my absence, so I kicked on the air. I took the printouts from my pocket and carefully unfolded them, spreading them out on the desk. The picture was an obvious photo opportunity before the failure since Marvin was smiling. I looked closely at Joyce Brenner and Timothy Ebersole. She really didn't appear to be the type who would get involved with somebody like Ebersole. Still, he was an attractive appearing gentleman and— he was rich.

The phone rang. I snapped up the receiver. "Hargro—"

"You were told to drop the case, Hargrove. Obviously you don't listen well or can't hear. You've been warned." CLICK.

There was no doubt in my mind who the person at the other end of this one-sided conversation was. *Exactly what are you trying to hide?* I thought. *What don't you want me to find out about your brother-in-law, Marvin, or even about you?*

I read the article, hoping to find the names of the four people in the background. It didn't take too long to find the line giving me that information.

... Dr. Landelli praised his staff consisting of Dr. Joyce Brenner, Dr. James Harbinger and their four interns: Linda Hoffman, Stephanie Zane, Ren Nin and Qiang Wong, for all their ...

I scribbled the names on my notepad, carefully re-folded the printout and stuck it into the blank file folder in my drawer and closed the drawer. The front door opened. Looking up, I noticed Marvin's brother-in-law and sister saunter into the office.

"Are you here to make good on the threat?" I asked nonchalantly, crossing my arms defiantly while easing back into my chair.

He scowled at me. "What are you talking about, Hargrove? I told you to drop the case, but I never threatened you."

It was my turn to frown. "What about the phone call from

you less than ten minutes ago?" I held up my hands and with the first two fingers on each hand making air quotation marks. "You've been warned."

"No idea what you're referring to," he said and let his wife sit in the chair. "We've come back to make amends. It seems somebody truly has robbed her brother and we want you to take the case."

"I've already taken the case from your brother." I picked up the pen from the desk and fiddled with it in my hands. "He's paid me and I plan to see it through." I hesitated and gave him a stern look. "And, I'm not scared of threats, either."

"Again, Hargrove, you've got me pegged all wrong. I didn't call you and I certainly didn't threaten you." He glanced about the room and spotted the folding chair against the wall, grabbed it, and sat beside his wife. "Look, Detective Hargrove. I know we got off on the wrong foot earlier, but we've been talking with Marvin, and decided he has the right to hire a detective, although we truly do believe he should have called the police."

"Except," Marvin's sister jumped in. "We don't know how he plans to pay you. My brother hasn't worked in several months." She rubbed her hands together nervously. "He's been sick."

"Wait a minute," I said softly. I needed to get a grasp of the whole situation. "Let's start this whole thing over. Who are you? I mean, what are your names?"

"My name is Georgiana Lashlin Morrison," she said then pointed at the man next to her. "And this is Henry Morrison, my husband."

I scribbled down the names. "Can I get an address and phone?" The paperwork was completed and I now knew who I was talking with.

"Well, Ms. Morrison, I—"

"Please call me Ms. Lashlin. Most people know me by that name since Henry and I have only been married five months."

"Fine," I replied. "You just stated your brother was sick. He told me about it while we had lunch earlier today."

"He told you about Dr. Landelli and his sessions?" Henry stared at me with definite surprise on his face.

I eased back. "He told me about his breakdown," I re-stated. "Who is Dr. Landelli?"

"That would be Dr. Marvin Landelli." Georgiana leaned in. "I've never met the man but he has been assisting my brother for several months now."

It was evident I didn't have all the facts and I wasn't about to fumble my way through this meeting with them. Yet, at the same time, I didn't want to let anything out of the bag, as if I had any idea what was in the bag.

"Can you tell me..." I leaned forward and put pen to paper. "Is your brother married and does he have any children?"

"Oh, heavens no," Georgiana said with a light laugh. "He is a sworn bachelor, never married."

"Fine." I placed a question mark behind the word 'son' I'd written. I'd get back to Landelli later. "What can you tell me about the theft. Is there anything to make his e-reader stand out from the other umpteen million out there?"

Georgiana fidgeted in the chair and pursed her lips in thought.

"Well, I've only seen it once," Henry started. "It is black and has a picture of Einstein on the back and he has fangs." He rolled his eyes. "I'm assuming Marvin scratched on the fangs, sort of like a vampire with dripping blood."

"How quaint," I said. "Very picturesque."

"That's on a removable cover," Georgiana added. "But he does have his name engraved on the back left bottom corner. Somebody would have to scratch it out or cover it in some manner." Once more she pursed her lips and frowned. "He said some flash drive was stolen and that they were stealing his project."

"Project?" My ears perked up. Until this moment they'd never once mentioned his work.

"Some delusion," Henry said, and glanced at his wife who was not watching him. He quickly made a circular motion at the temple and shrugged.

"He claims he's been working for some big technological company." She frowned, pursed her lips, and then dabbed at her eyes before shaking her head. "He... he's been sick and I know for a fact he hasn't worked in a very long time." Georgiana paused and stared at the desk. "I called, you know." Her words were a mere whisper. "I called the place he claimed he worked." She inhaled deeply. "They've never heard of Marvin Lashlin. When I confronted Marvin with this, he said his project is so secret, most people don't know he works there." She shook her head. "Sadly, he doesn't leave his apartment."

"I see," I said. I didn't see anything but it made for conversation. "So, how do you know this to be a fact?"

"Simple," Georgiana said. "When I spoke with the apartment manager, Russ, he told me the only person going in and out of my brother's apartment is Dr. Landelli. Russ said he hasn't seen my brother come out of the apartment."

"Does this Russ have a last name?" I hovered my pen over my pad, waiting.

"Just a second," she said and pulled out her phone. She played with for a few seconds. "Ah, here it is — Russell White. Would you like his phone number?"

I nodded my head as I scribbled the name.

"It is 212-555-5244. He manages the Brighton Apartments."

"Thank you. I may have to get in touch with him later." I stabbed a period after apartment.

"Is there anything else we can help you with?" Henry stood. "Damned chair gets hard and I hate sitting for any great length of time."

"You two have been very helpful. I may be getting in touch with Marvin for a few more details and see his apartment. Maybe my old police days might pick up on something he missed."

Georgiana stood and the two of them sauntered out of my office, waving at the door as they left, this time much friendlier than the earlier tirade-ridden exit. Now I had to call Willie to see if he would give me info over the phone on the new names I had. I shook my head. All I had to do was pay the fee and I could have my own terminal and do this research myself. I silently laughed... *Just pay the fee*.

20

#

Williamson was in a much nicer mood on the phone and read me off the details. The girls were clean, but Ren Nin and Qiang Wong had rap sheets. Both had run-ins with the local police, and while they claimed natural citizenship in San Francisco, neither had supporting documents to prove it. Qiang Wong had noted affiliations with a tong named The Blue Lotus Society. I quickly noted that and then was surprised to hear Henry Morrison was clean, not even a blip on the radar. His wife, though, had a notation of a minor scuffle involving a family dispute with her brother.

There was silence on the phone for a few moments. I frowned trying to figure out what was happening since I could hear the background sounds of the precinct and could also tell Williamson wasn't talking to anyone. "Hello? You still there Willie?"

"Uh, Barry, you said you went to Chang's today. Did you notice anything different?" Williamson's voice was low and conspiratorial. "Did anyone say anything about Chang?"

"I asked Mai Lin about some Mongolian food and she said Chang had been out for the last few days. She thought he was sick. What gives?"

"You're the mastermind who usually puts all the loose ends together, you tell me. I got a call this morning from Ren Nin. His uncle has been missing for the last three days. Before you ask, yes, his uncle is Chang. Then about two hours later, homicide tells me Chang has been found dead. Needless to say, you show up asking about people who are involved in my case. So, now I'm asking... you got any clues?"

That was a lot of information and I started to mull it over in my head.

"You're being very quiet, Barry. This is your good buddy, Willie. Remember me? We've been partners for years... if you have something, share it with me."

"Listen, Willie. I only went to Chang's for lunch to meet with a client. My client had an item stolen. In my research I found Ren Nin in a photograph and it appears he works at E-MIT-C. Otherwise I have nothing regarding Chang's demise. I'm sorry buddy, but—"

"Fine," Williamson snapped. "You don't want to share, so be it. Don't bother calling me for any more information. This is supposed to be a two-way street and you just made it a one-way dead end."

He slammed the phone down without even a chance of rebuttal.

I sat there with the receiver to my ear, shocked, again listening to a dial tone.

CHAPTER FOUR

I hung up the phone and pondered my next move. It was then I decided a visit to the resident manager of Marvin's apartment complex was in order. Russell White. He seemed to have a pulse on the comings and goings of my mysterious Marvin. *Sometimes it is better to start with the hired help*, I thought.

A short, brisk walk brought me to Marvin's apartment building and I was pressing the button marked 'Resident Manager' and hearing Mr. White's gruff voice. Moments later found me inside his apartment.

If he'd been shorter, thinner and mousier, Russ would have been what I expected, but he wasn't. Russ could probably stretch his body up to six feet when needed, had a slight paunch and probably was a bouncer or biker in his younger hey-days. The fitted t-shirt was too big at the shoulders and too tight at the stomach and definitely too short on length since it didn't meet the well-worn, faded and ripped blue jeans he wore. The drooping white belly flesh was not what I wanted to see.

Russ kicked back in his beat-up, green tweed lounger and lifted a sweating bottle of beer. "You want one?"

I gave it a second's thought then nodded. "Sure, I'm the boss and I don't plan to fire me."

He put his drink down, reached over the far side of his chair and lifted a bottle from what I could only assume to be a cooler. He wiped the bottle dry with a towel, kicked forward, leaned over to hand it to me and finally returned to his reclining position, grabbing his bottle once more. He slugged down a few gulps with a resounding 'ah' afterward. At least the paunch was explained.

I popped the lid and slammed down a healthy guzzle. The cold liquid was refreshing.

"So Elizabeth Morri—" I coughed to clear my throat. "Lashlin," I corrected myself. "I understand she has you keeping tabs on her brother. Is that correct?"

"From my seat here..." He leaned over to glance out the

window. "I can see everyone who comes and goes."

I heard the door slam shut through the thin walls.

"Or, at least hear, if nothing else. There goes Mrs. Heffelstauffer with her English bulldog. None of the residents are allowed pets, but she pays me an extra fifty each month to keep it. The other residents don't bitch, and management doesn't care." He smiled, the missing left canine tooth gaped wide as he lifted his beer into the air like a toast. "I keep the extra."

"I see," I replied. "Like the setup between you and Mrs. Lashlin."

"Hey, if the woman wants to pay me to keep tabs on her brother, who am I not to help her out for a small fee?" He rubbed his thumb against the index and long finger.

It didn't take much of an imagination to realize this man had a booming enterprise on the side. "So tell me, how many times has her brother left the apartment in the last two weeks?"

"Never seen the man," Russ replied. "He stays inside constantly. But…" He touched the side of his nose. "He is visited by that Dr. Landelli every day like clockwork." He took a swig. "With Landelli you can almost set a watch. Every day, out at 8 A.M. and back by 5:30 P.M."

The beer was refreshing and my mind started to feel the effects of the alcohol. Not that I was getting drunk, but I was starting to feel warm.

The alarm went off inside my brain.

"You mean, in at eight and out by five thirty, right?" *Landelli comes to visit him*, I thought.

"No, I figure this doctor guy comes in before I start in the morning and leaves after I've closed the drapes at night. I really do have a life beyond sitting here all day. I'm a resident manager not a twenty-four hour guard."

Suddenly this lug's words made sense. Dr. Landelli visited on his way to the office and again on his way home. Again, a niggling of my memories started to bother me. Something wasn't quite right.

"Did you see Marvin Lashlin leave today? Say a little before noon?"

"I doubt it." Russ sat there with a silly grin. "From sometime around eleven until noon, give or take a little, that's my personal constitution moment during the day."

I raised my eyebrows with a quizzical look.

He downed the last his beer. "I grab a book or magazine and head for the crapper."

"So... Mr. Lashlin *could* leave and come back without your knowing." I took another satisfying gulp. "Therefore, you're not constantly watching the doorway."

"Of course not! I'm not a total perv," Russ said and grabbed another beer. "In fact, I usually nap a little in the afternoon."

Nap? More likely passed out in a drunken stupor.

It was a whim, but I decided to see what came of it. I pulled the folded newspaper picture I had of Dr. Landelli. I handed it over to Russ. "Is this Dr. Landelli?"

"Yup, that's the guy. Dr. Landelli. He is here every day to help Mr. Lashlin with his rehabilitation."

Now I was totally confused and prayed it wasn't the beer playing with my mind. *Why would a bio-neurogenesist treat, or be involved with a basket case like Lashlin?*

My head started to spin. The beer was almost empty so I carefully placed it on the table next to me. My mind raced. Dr. Landelli and Marvin Lashlin both looked like each other. I closed my eyes.

"You okay, Detective?"

"I'm fine," I answered and opened my eyes. I took a deep breath and ran my hands across the top of my head, pushing back the hair. "I guess I should be going. Thank you for the information." I stood and headed for the door.

"Don't mind me, detective," Russ slurred. "I'm staying put."

I shut the door behind me, gazed up the stairs and debated visiting Marvin. I decided against it. There was no doubt my breath smelled of beer and right now I didn't want to face what my mind was screaming at me—Lashlin and Landelli were the same person. I wanted to think maybe separated twins at birth, but there was the younger sister. I headed home, stopping at *Jingle's Bar and Grill*, the popular police hangout and listened to the gossip there.

In the morning light things had a different view. I smiled. The idea of twins played in my head and I could deal with that. Flipping my notepad open, I jotted down a reminder to ask Miss Lashlin if adoption was a possibility regarding her brother.

The phone rang. It was Williamson.

"Sorry about yesterday, Barry."

"No problem," I replied. "I know I intrude and push where I shouldn't."

"No, really," Willie said. "It was my fault. I was just intensely involved with my case regarding Mr. Chang." His voice lowered. "Did you know all the blood in his body had been drained?"

Not only did my ears prick up at the words, my eyebrows lifted up in anticipation. This was juicy gossip and I was amazed I'd not heard it last night at *Jingles*, especially after seeing two of the precinct's largest blabbermouths loosening up there.

"Surprisingly, no I didn't know," I whispered back. "Preston was at *Jingles* and that big mouth never mentioned it."

"Just found out myself this morning," Willie said. "Got the full autopsy barely twenty minutes ago and it —"

The phone was silent.

"What?" I practically screamed into the phone. "Don't leave me hanging, Willie."

"Hush. I'll be back in a second."

I listened to voices mumbling and talking in the background. It was obvious to me Willie was listening to some shop talk and it had to be important.

"You're not going to believe this, Barry," Willie whispered into the phone. "Another body was found and it was drained, too. A young woman, this time. They're thinking we've got some sick vampire wannabe on the loose."

"What the hell?" It was the only thing I could mumble. The whole idea of draining a body of blood boggled my mind. Draining

26

two was unfathomable. My mind raced trying to figure out how any of my people could possibly be connected to this? I suddenly felt very sorry for Mr. Chang.

"You still there, Barry?"

"Yeah," I replied absently then reacted. "Think your lovely bride would enjoy a working meal tonight instead of Friday?"

"Let's keep it on for Friday since our babysitter would have to be home early — school, you know." There was a click on the phone, somebody had picked up. "Tell you what, how about we do lunch?" Willie said. "I'll take a long lunch since I need to check out things over at Changs. How about eleven-fortyish?"

"Sounds like a plan," I said. "See you then." I slid the phone silently into the cradle. I wondered who had picked up on the line. I was sure Willie was checking on that right now.

I looked at my watch — a little over a two hour wait until Willie and I met. Until then I decided it would be in my best interest to check into Marvin's co-workers at E-MIT-C and see if I could ascertain who stole the stuff from his apartment.

A pain-staking call to the personnel department at E-MIT-C had me near pulling my hairs out. Finally, in desperation, I pulled out Marvin Landelli's card and called his number.

"Dr. Landelli's office. This is Dr. Joyce Brenner. May I help you?"

"My name is Barry Hargrove. Is Dr. Landelli in today? If so, may I speak with him?"

"Certainly." The phone went silent.

I was intrigued. Dr. Landelli was working, but then again, it seemed proper.

"Detective Hargrove," Landelli snapped into the phone. "I certainly hope this is good news. Have you been able to retrieve Lashlin's lost item?"

"Actually, doctor, I'm being stymied at the personnel office. Something about the director being out and interviews being kept to a minimum. Would it be possible to circumvent them and get me in to speak with your staff?"

"So, you haven't found it yet." There was a long moment of

27

silence. "Please be here by no later than 2 p.m. and I will allow you to speak with the people in my department." Again there was silence. "Personally, I don't see why you are wasting time interviewing my staff, but if you feel you must play that particular game, so be it. I will have them at your disposal. Good day, sir."

Once more I sat there with a dial tone humming in my ear. He was a very short tempered man, but I had my interview with some of the people I wanted. Of course, the big cheese, Tim Ebersole would be the most difficult person to pin down. I smiled. I'd see him, but all in due time.

I still had time so I decided I would follow up on what I'd told Marvin's sister. I'd check out his apartment to see if I could find any possible clues of the theft.

As I flipped the lock on the door I heard the thunder and felt the old building shudder. *Crap! It's raining*, I thought. Fortunately I hadn't pulled the door closed so I reached in and grabbed the huge, black umbrella leaning just inside the door. A gust of wind from the spring thunderstorm pulled at the umbrella as I opened it outside. It was only a couple of blocks to Marvin's place and I made the trip quickly with the wind pushing me while the umbrella pulled me most of the way there.

I saw Russ sitting in his green lounger as I climbed the stairs and waved at him. The buzzer was sounding as I pushed the door open. He stood at his door, waiting.

"Just going up to see Mr. Lashlin," I said while closing up the umbrella and knocking most of the rainwater onto the extra rug he'd put down for the storm.

Russ was about to say something, hesitated then spoke. "He should be up there, 2-C, he never leaves." Russ grimaced, stepped back into his apartment, and the door closed.

I plodded up the stairs to the second floor where Marvin's apartment was. I stared at the two unadorned doors, 2-A, 2-B. Grey tweed carpeting led me down the plain hallway to 2-C and 2-D. I knocked on the steel door.

"Leave me alone."

It was Marvin Lashlin's mousey voice.

"It's Detective Hargrove, Mr. Lashlin. We need to discuss some things."

There was no response. I waited and finally knocked again.

"Go away. Leave me alone."

"Mr. Lashlin," I started. "We really need to talk."

No response.

"Mr. Lashlin?" I knocked on the door.

"Leave me alone. Go away. I'm busy."

"I can play this game all day, Mr. Lashlin." I knocked on the door.

"Leave me alone."

"I need to talk to you." Again I rapped on the door.

"Go away. Leave me alone."

"Fine, Mr. Lashlin. I will have your sister address this with you later."

There was no response. I waited, leaned in and listened. There was absolutely no sound of activity from the other side of the door. I shook my head and headed back down the dingy hallway.

Russ stood at the doorway as I came down the stairs.

"I could have told you he doesn't open the door during the day, but I figured you'd still go up."

There was no way for me to control the smile I had. He was right, I'd still had gone up. I glanced at my watch. I could join Russ for a beer – he had one already in hand – or head over to Chang's. The restaurant won — green tea wouldn't leave me drunk, or have a residual tell-tale scent.

CHAPTER FIVE

It was too early for Willie to show, but I headed over to Chang's nonetheless. As I approached, my mind immediately wondered if they'd be closed. My fretting was for naught, they were open. I pushed the big, red door with one of the golden dragons open and entered. It was somber.

"Nǐhǎo, Mei Lin," I said.

"Mr. Hargrove," she said. Her eyes lighted and I saw they were swollen and puffy; she'd been crying. "You hear Mr. Chang dead?"

I nodded my head solemnly. "Can I get a table in a corner, away from others? Sgt Williamson will be joining me."

Mei Lin pointed to a booth in the corner where the only traffic would be the wait staff.

"That will be perfect," I said and headed toward it. "Some ginger tea, please?"

"Shì." Mei Lin nodded and hustled away.

I sat there going over my notes and realizing the very little I'd accomplished so far this morning. Willie slipped in the back door and stood there shaking the rain off him.

"It's coming down like cow peeing a rock out there." Williamson slid into the booth. He pushed a plastic packet across the table toward me. "See what you think and don't let anyone see." He glanced about. "It would be my ass if I was caught showing you that."

I felt my eyebrows knit as I frowned at him. "What is this?"

"Among other things, it is Chang's autopsy. Plus, there is a picture of the new victim."

I carefully opened the package and removed the contents making sure nothing got wet. I laid the picture on the table and opened the report.

"Cause of death, exsanguination." I mumbled the words. My eyes roved the report. "My God," I exclaimed. "Less than eight ounces of blood remained? Damaged arm where it appears the hypodermic extraction was hastily ripped out?" I glanced at Willie. "What kind of shit is this?"

"One very sick perp out there." Willie nodded at the picture. "She was the same, injured arm."

Mei Lin came up with a new pot of tea and to take orders before I had a chance to hide the picture of the latest victim. "Luli," she whispered, her eyes wide, staring at the picture. "That Luli."

"You know her?" Willie asked.

Mei Lin nodded, a tear welling in her eye to finally trace a path down her pale cheek. "She work here. No come in today." She wiped the tear away with her hand and took a deep breath. "You order now?"

"When are they going to close the restaurant?" I asked.

"We close 3 p.m. today. Mr. Chang's number one son, Bingwen, he say close restaurant for three weeks of proper mourning. Funeral Monday."

Willie's cell phone buzzed. He glanced at it. "A text from the office," he said, glanced at Mei Lin then back down, and pointed at the menu. "I'll have Happy Family with white rice, one egg roll, and a bowl of wonton soup." He looked up at the young Oriental girl and smiled. "Could you have them kick in a little heat? Make it a little hot?"

She nodded.

"Make mine Kung Pao Beef, fried rice, two egg rolls and a bowl of hot and sour soup." I glanced up at her. "You know I want it hot, the more, the better."

Mei Lin nodded again and scurried away.

Williamson clicked buttons on the phone. "The office said they've found another body."

"Three of them?" I whispered. "What is this creep up to?"

"They established time of death on this one to be about the same as Chang's. The weird part, his body was found only two blocks from Chang's. Another young person, a boy, Caucasian, about seventeen years old. Again, ripped up arm and lacking blood content." Williamson shook his head.

"The truly strange part is the connection between my case

and your case. I have a stolen electronic device, a weird-ass hermit who has an even stranger doctor. The doctor's lab assistants seem to be the connection factor. Just who are Qiang Wong and Ren Nin? What is their tong up to?"

"Why is your client so adamant about getting back a stupid electronic gadget? He can buy another one so cheaply." Willie shuffled the papers back together to put them in the plastic bag. "It doesn't make any sense."

Mei Lin put the bowls of soup and egg rolls down on the table along with fried noodles. "Bingwen want to know how Luli die."

"Tell you what, Mei Lin," Willie offered. "I'll finish my meal and then come back to talk with Bingwen and you. Is that okay?"

"Shì." Once more she politely nodded and scurried away.

"This has become one shit job." Willie slurped broth. "I enjoy working Missing Persons but it is much nicer when the M.P. is alive. This homicide stuff is shit, exciting, but shit work, nonetheless."

"Join me," I offered. "Not great pay, but it is a living."

Mei Lin hurried to the table with the plates of food. She placed the mixture of chicken, pork, beef, lobster, shrimp, scallops and chopped veggies in front of Williamson. I could see the small flecks of red chili flakes sprinkled through the mixture. It was hot. Mei Lin then placed the platter filled with steak strips slathered in a thick, dark sauce over a mixture of water chestnuts, peppers, onions and well defined pieces of red chili peppers. A small pile of peanuts garnished the top. My mouth started to salivate at the prospect.

"Bingwen say talk later yes. No bill. Free meal." She blurted the words, turned and was gone before we could say a thing.

"Enjoy your meal," I said and scooped a huge helping onto a fork. My phone rang.

"This is Detective Hargrove," I snapped into the mouthpiece as I chewed.

"Eating! I'm not paying you to continually eat at Chang's," Dr. Landelli sneered. "Something has come up and you will need to be at my office no later than half past one. If you leave now, you will make it."

I frowned and glanced around the restaurant. He couldn't be

in here and I didn't see anyone I recognized or associated with him. The only person who could have known would be Russ back at the apartment for Marvin Lashlin, and that didn't make any sense.

"You're wasting time, detective. You'd best get a hustle on."

"I'll be there," I snarled and snapped the phone shut, hanging up on him. The food was great, what food I could taste as I scooped it into my mouth and swallowed most of it whole. "I have to go now," I garbled at Willie between scoops. "I need to be at E-MIT-C by one thirty." A few forkfuls of fried rice made my mouth, but I left most of it on the plate. Grabbing the two egg rolls, I headed out the door. "Catch you later," I sputtered, rice flying through the air from my mouth.

* * *

A couple of blocks later found me walking across the street from Brighton Apartment. Whatever possessed me to glance up, I have no idea, but I did. My mind wandered and I considered the building's structure and where Marvin Lashlin's apartment was located. It would be this side, to the back. Somebody stood at the window looking out at me. I couldn't ascertain if it was a man or woman, but they never moved. It was like that person's eyes were following me. I felt a shiver enwrap its fingers around my spine and slither out my arms. Goosebumps sprouted all over my body. Without realizing, my pace picked up, and although I wasn't running, I was walking quicker than normal to get away. The subway was in the middle of the next block and I felt relief as I rounded the corner of the entrance. I glanced back. It appeared the person was still in the window, watching me.

The subway ride was uneventful and filled with the regular denizens of the system — tourists, crying kids, harried parents, homeless people, wasted minds both young and old, workers, and dreamers. My mind wandered as I listened to the repeating pattern of the ride. I shivered as I once more thought about the person standing in the window of Marvin's apartment. The image was vivid, burned into my memory.

The subway lurched then stopped. I looked around, this wasn't a scheduled stop. Most of the passengers continued with whatever it was they were doing. The tourists quickly donned nervous looks and gawked about.

I stood and started for a doorway while nonchalantly gazing out the window at the dark tunnel. *Subways don't stop in the middle of a tunnel for no reason*, I thought. *Usually they slow to a stop — not lurch to non-movement.* I continued to amble forward when the train suddenly lurched again. I stumbled, almost losing my balance and almost falling into the lap of an obese female stranger. I fumbled to apologize. Slowly the cars moved forward and I saw the flashing lights on the tunnel walls. The subway inched forward and as everyone glanced out the windows, flashlights flickered along the car and I could see police standing near the walls. The subway car pitched again and then picked up speed. Less than a minute later we slowed for the official stop. I got off to a reserved greeting of cops.

Police officers directed all departing passengers to the exit. I was probably one of the few who noticed there were no passengers getting on the subway.

"What's going on, officer?" I decided to ask a policeman who stood there aimlessly waving his flashlight, directing us out of the station.

"Nothing to concern yourself with, sir," the young cop replied. "Just a recon team."

I smiled at the young cop, shrugged, and followed the others out.

Recon? I knew better than that since I'd seen the shoe prints near the platform stairs. My mind raced at the possibilities. *Those prints looked like red mud and we don't have red dirt here.*

Exiting the subway entrance, I was greeted with a bright sun — the rain was gone. A mild spring breeze blew and as I turned, it gusted against my back on the short walk to my destination, E-MIT-C. I quickly realized I was backtracking the subway's path as I ambled toward E-MIT-C and could feel the next subway traveling beneath as it vibrated the sidewalk.

CHAPTER SIX

The lobby was elegant, a lot of glass, shiny metal, and light oak wood trim. E-MIT-C oozed modern. I strolled to one of the two women sitting behind the semi-circle reception area. The bleach-blond continued to talk into her microphone, yet gave me a pleasant smile. The brunette had her full attention on me.

"May I help you?" It was the perfect voice, soft, not meek, but not demanding, and very clear.

"Barry Hargrove," I said. "I have an appointment with Dr. Landelli." I was expecting problems and just by the way the receptionist wrinkled her nose, I knew I wouldn't be disappointed.

"Are you sure he is expecting you?" She scanned her monitor. "I don't have anything in my records indicating any visitors for him today."

"It was a last minute thing," I replied. "Call him, if you don't believe me." *You're cute and well trained*, I thought. *But I can play my trump card and call Landelli if needed.*

She glanced at her companion who barely shrugged while raising her eyebrows to indicate she had no idea either.

"I'll buzz him, sir." She had to be nice, but I quickly ascertained for some strange reason all public interaction seemed to be at a standstill.

I watched as she nonchalantly placed a finger to her headset and eased her microphone closer to her lips. She whispered and turned slightly away from me to make sure I couldn't hear or, was I paranoid, read her lips. She turned back and looked up at me.

"He will be with you momentarily. Have a seat, please." She motioned to the couches and chairs by the windows. Once more the aura of assurance flowed from her and she was in command.

I'd barely had a chance to sit when Landelli charged into the lobby.

"Detective Hargrove, how wonderful." He grabbed my hand, shook it and then gently grabbed my elbow while easing me toward the closing door. "Come with me."

"Dr. Landelli," the receptionist called.

He turned momentarily toward her. "It's quite all right, Sherry." Landelli ushered me through the heavy wooden doors and into the sanctum sanctorum of Ebersole Micro Intra-Techtonics Corporation.

"This way," Landelli whispered and took the lead. "The second door on the right."

By the time he'd told me where we were headed, he was shoving the frosted double glass doors open.

I stumbled into the room and quickly realized it to be a maze of absolute horror for any person with aichmophobia, let alone trypanophobia, which I had. I was a klutz and those closest to me knew it. There were too many pointed objects and needles everywhere, but it was the medical procedures involving what I could only guess to be volunteer patients that scared me the most. I gazed at arms stretched out with IVs and other apparatus, tubing ran in every direction: some red, some clear. My body stiffened, a chilling curl crawled down my spine and the sweats began in drastic contrast to the chills.

"Are you okay," Dr. Landelli asked and grabbed my arm in a useless gesture.

I felt my body weakening and saw two aides drop their hypodermics to move quickly toward me. My body collapsed into their arms as I succumbed to the darkness of my mind.

"Detective Hargrove? Barry?"

The voice was distant, but the stench of ammonia had me breathing with a scrunched nose and tears filling my eyes.

Dr. Landelli smiled at me. "You gave us a good start, detective. I don't believe I've ever met anyone with such a severe case of trypanophobia before."

"Most people think it is aichmophobia," I muttered and sheepishly grinned back the doctor.

I sat and looked about. A curtain encircled me much like

emergency rooms have and I could hear people beyond.

"Where am I?"

"You're still in my lab," Landelli replied. He kept an eye on me, observing my actions. "Off in a corner where you won't hurt yourself."

"Might as well open the curtains," I said. "Now that I know it is there, I'm a little better prepared." I kicked my feet over the edge of the gurney. "Bring it on."

An intern slowly opened the curtain and revealed the lab once more. I counted the people standing, staring in my direction. Fourteen. Suddenly an applause began with one person clapping, others followed. I could feel my cheeks warming in embarrassment.

"We don't normally get this much drama," Landelli said and slapped me on the back. "I'm sure you want to get your work done. Who do you want to question first?"

I grabbed my notepad and flipped the pages. "Is Dr. Joyce Brenner here today?"

"Yes," a young woman said from behind me.

"If you like," Landelli started. "We can leave this curtain more closed than open and you could use it as an office."

I jumped off the gurney and grabbed two chairs. "That would work just fine." I placed the two chairs across from each other. I glanced around for Dr. Brenner. "If you would be so kind," I asked and offered her a chair.

The others drifted away and I was alone with a very attractive young lady. The picture from the newspaper did not flatter her in any way. It was total injustice. I sat in the chair opposite her.

"Just a couple of questions, Dr. Brenner." I opened the clipping I had and turned it so she could see it. "Can you tell me what the assistants were doing at this point in time?"

She leaned over and suddenly I smelled a mixture of jasmine and vanilla. The fragrance was very subtle. Her fingers took the paper and she pulled it closer to view. She frowned. "It would appear they are fumbling with the boggle on the do-whacker." She looked up at me and waited.

"Excuse me? Boggle? Do-whacker?" I pointed at the picture.

"Are those scientific terms?"

"No. I could have said hematological mistifier on the bio-amino exchange automaton. Would that have made it any clearer?"

I did exactly what every man does when he meets a woman with more knowledge than him, I scratched my head, grimaced a smile, and nodded my head. I'd been put in my place, but I still wasn't down.

"So, would fiddling with the boggle have caused the do-whacker to fail?"

She smiled. "Not really. I was there when the demonstration failed. The exchanger worked fine until it was required to..." She glanced at the picture again. "Strange. I never thought about it, but if the boggle was the wrong one, it would have failed."

I frowned. "Exactly what do you mean by 'wrong one' when you said that?"

"Dr. Landelli had finalized the prototype." She bowed her head and placed her folded hands with index fingers together up to her lips and thought quietly. "If an older hematological mistifier had been used in place of the new one, the—" She looked up at me with a wide-eyed expression. "Dr. Landelli was right when he said he had been sabotaged." Dr. Brenner snapped the paper from my hands and once more scrutinized the image. "I've never trusted Qiang Wong."

"Just one more thing," I said to calm her down. "Do you have any ideas of who may have stolen Mr. Lashlin's reader?"

"Who?"

"Mr. Marvin Lashlin? He worked here a while back, had a breakdown? Remember him?"

She slowly shook her head. "I don't recall anyone with that name ever working here. I've been here for almost ten years."

"Thank you," I mumbled, slightly confused by her response. My mind raced remembering Lashlin's words. Even his sister said he had worked here. I attempted to rationalize — this was a big place and obviously Dr. Brenner didn't know everyone who worked here. "Guess I need to talk with Qiang Wong next."

"I'll get him," Dr. Brenner offered, her voice a pleasant bouquet of flowers.

On a whim I glanced down at her hands. She was married. I watched her stand and walk toward the curtain.

"Qiang!" She snarled as she pulled the curtain back. "Over here! Now!"

I practically jumped out of my skin, being startled and surprised by her voice. She'd been so soft and demure while talking to me and now she screamed like a banshee at the hired help. It appeared her patience had a very low tolerance level. "Move it!" Dr. Brenner turned back and smiled at me. "He'll be here shortly," she whispered and disappeared beyond the curtain.

The Oriental man came around the corner of the room, his eyes were afire with anger and hate while he glared in the direction of Dr. Brenner. He grabbed the edge of the curtain and I heard the fabric snap at the action. His dark eyes appraised me and I could feel his distrust immediately.

"Mr. Wong," I said, standing and offering my hand to shake.

He placed his hands together and bowed to me. I returned the gesture then offered him a chair.

"How long have you worked here?" I asked and once more flipped through my notepad to find a blank page. I sat.

"I stand. Two years." He reached into his large lab coat pocket and pulled out an electronic device which he started to manipulate with finger actions.

"Can you tell me what you're doing in this picture?" I held out the photograph and pointed to him with the apparatus.

"Clean lens." His eyes barely flicked to notice what I held. He continued to play with the device. It was then I noticed the silver scratches and major gouges on the bottom left hand corner of the black item.

"My friend has something like that," I said casually with a laugh in my voice. "He lost it recently. Maybe you've heard of him, his name is Marvin Lashlin." My eyes were trained on him.

He froze momentarily then he reacted. The reader dropped and skidded across the floor. Qiang's lab coat floated in the air like a convoluted parachute. The man was out of my area and headed for the door.

"Stop him!" It was Dr. Brenner. She pointed at the escaping Qiang as he zigzagged around the patients, lab techs, tables, and equipment.

He cleared the obstacles and was on the homestretch to the double doors and freedom. It was perfect timing, like a comedy routine in a movie, the left front door slammed open catching Qiang full frontal. He shifted backwards into the air to collapse onto the floor.

"Dr. Landelli!" The entering person shouted, never realizing what service he had committed. The reaction was slow and he finally turned to see Qiang on the floor.

Three lab assistants quickly had Qiang in their grips as he struggled to get free. If he truly belonged to a tong, he was obviously the weak link since I saw no indication of any martial arts.

"Dr. Landelli. You need to see this!" It was the new person.

"What is your problem, Mr. Nusbaum?" Landelli moved forward and once more I saw the disdainful attitude the man could exhibit. "By the way, thanks for stopping Qiang." He glanced at me. "Although I'm still not sure why." He cocked a questioning eye again in my direction then gave the newcomer his full attention.

"They just arrested Dr. Harbinger. Did you know he had a lab downstairs in the basement?"

Landelli glanced around. "What do you mean, arrested? He was here just a few minutes ago."

"He left to get something," Dr. Brenner offered. "You were on your way to get Detective Hargrove. He and I were talking when you said we'd be questioned. Dr. Harbinger said he had to go get his notes and left shortly after you."

"Why'd they arrest him?" Once more Landelli took command and I waited anxiously for the answer.

Nusbaum stood there nervously wringing his hands, his eyes wide with fear. "Can you imagine what this will do to us? The scandal?"

"Why?" Landelli demanded and grabbed the man's shoulders.

"They found blood in the subway system and were able to trace it back to a lab we didn't even know existed in our basement.

40

When they broke down the door, Dr. Harbinger was inside. They grabbed his reader which he had clutched close to him. He kept screaming at them 'Not fair' which I have no idea what it means."

The reader! My mind was alert and I dodged back to the curtained area. The device wasn't on the floor where Qiang had dropped it. I scanned the area hoping it might have gotten kicked into a corner or perhaps picked up and left on a table. It hadn't. Once more it was lost when it had been so close, almost within my grasp.

CHAPTER SEVEN

I stood like a museum statue in the curtained room, analyzing my next move.

"If you look for reader, he no steal." The voice caught me off guard. "Qiang buy from thief in alley three months ago. You want Qiang's reader?"

There, in his hands, he held the device out to me. I carefully took it, turned it over and looked at the damage in the left hand corner. Although the gouging and scratching was severe, there was no doubt in my mind the first letter was a scrolled "B" which was nothing resembling an "M" for Marvin or "L" for Lashlin. I frowned. *Why did Qiang bolt?* The thought was foremost in my mind.

"You frown, detective," Ren said. "I work for Dr. Landelli. Qiang work for Dr. Harbinger. He help Dr. Landelli."

"Do you think Qiang knew about Dr. Harbinger's secret lab?"

Ren nodded in agreement. "He know. I know." He glanced at me with surprise on his face. Immediately he began to shake his hands in denial. "I go to find Qiang — he gone. Him hiding. Qiang tell me he have secret place, but no tell me where."

"Has Qiang ever told you what he did for Dr. Harbinger?"

Ren shook his head then cautiously peeked at the contraption sitting in the corner.

My eyes followed in the direction he stared, my spine shivered. In the darkness, partially covered with a tarp, the monster lurked, waiting. It was the device — the one from the newspaper clipping which was Dr. Landelli's folly and failure.

"Do you know what it does?"

Again he shook his head in denial before slowly beginning to nod.

I leaned in. "What?" I whispered.

"Pure blood," Ren replied. "It make pure blood."

Landelli slapped me on the back, startling me since I hadn't seen him approach. "Ah, Detective Hargrove, has there been enough excitement around here for you today?" He glanced over at Rin. "So

42

what have you two been discussing?"

"What your machine does," I replied nonchalantly. "Pure blood?"

Landelli snickered. "That is a very simplistic explanation. My machine takes a small amount of a person's blood, cleanses it and returns it back into the blood stream."

"You mean like a kidney dialysis machine?"

"Very similar," the little doctor replied while hedging his answer. "My machine doesn't worry about urea or salt in the blood, although if it is there, it does remove it. No, this monstrosity is supposed to purge all impurities from the blood stream." He stood there with a smug smile. "Sort of like a rejuvenation process but in small segments, not more than a half liter of blood at a time."

I nodded my head as if I understood, it always made the client feel comfortable.

"It appears my protégé had grander aspirations." He grabbed my elbow. "Come with me." He looked at the young Chinese man. "You, too, Ren. Your friend, Qiang, was involved much too deeply in Dr. Harbinger's strange mad-scientist lab."

Dr. Landelli led us through hallways, a couple of stairwells and then we were in a taped-off police investigation area.

"Beyond that yellow tape, Dr. Harbinger performed some very bizarre experiments. I glanced over at Ren who twitched and stood awkwardly watching.

"It seems Dr. Harbinger was attempting to perform a full blood transfusion using a young person."

My mind flashed with an image of Luli and her ripped arm. I shivered at the prospect of all the tubes, needles and equipment to perform something of that caliber. A strange and perverted thought entered my mind.

"Dr. Landelli, could this machine be used to purge the blood of a young person and then transfer it to an older person?"

The man's eyes flickered about as he thought. "The feasibility is possible but I would think the best potential of such a feat would be only a fifty percent mixture."

"Fifty percent?" I questioned.

"Folks," the cop started. I recognized him from the subway station as he approached. "This isn't a tourist stop or stage show. Please move along. I'm sure Mr. Ebersole is paying you to work, not gawk." He spread his arms out in an attempt to shoo us away.

"Let's resume this discussion back in my office," Landelli offered.

"Dr. Landelli," Tim Nusbaum called. "I need you in my office for a few questions, if you don't mind." He nodded at me. "Could you come back tomorrow to finish whatever business you have?"

I shook my head affirmatively.

"I show you out," Ren said. "This way." He took the lead, quietly and quickly moving through the maze of hallways and stairwells.

Along the way I heard bits and pieces of the rumors being discussed and listened to the small segments of conversations: ...a leaking drain pipe with blood... ...a frickin' fountain of youth... ...secret laboratory with a mad scientist... ...left hand doesn't know what the right... ...people died in his experiments... ...poor Marvin, he never knew...

My ears picked out the 'Marvin' mention and wondered who would call Dr. Landelli by his first name. Even Dr. Brenner never referred to him that way. I attempted to glance back at the group but I couldn't ascertain exactly who said it. The group consisted of about six women.

Suddenly, like being hit by a truck, I realized what Mr. Nusbaum had said early on. The words blazed in my mind. *They grabbed the reader he clutched...*

"Ren! Can you take me back to the scene?"

He frowned, questioning my motives. "Now?"

"Yes, now," I replied and had his sleeve and was pulling him with me back the way we'd come. "I just realized Dr. Harbinger had a reader." I glanced eagerly at the young lab assistant. "It might be the one I'm looking for."

"Police evidence," Ren said flatly. "You go. Come back tomorrow." He stopped and now pulled me toward the double doors I'd come in earlier with Dr. Landelli. He was much stronger than I thought and he appeared.

"I need to see that reader," I pleaded.

"Tomorrow." Ren insisted.

The door opened and I found myself in the bright lobby with a couple of police officers sternly glaring at me as Ren pushed me through.

"Is there a problem?" the shorter of the two officers asked.

"No," I replied, straightened my jacket and headed for the exit door. "See you tomorrow, Sherry." I waved at the brunette and she sheepishly grinned and waved back.

# # #

"Lie, dammit," I growled under my breath at Willie. I was irked and tired. Yesterday's little incident at E-MIT-C left me anxious and wanting answers. I had only one desire. "We need to get our hands on that reader."

Willie gazed over at me. "We? I think it is more you than me."

I wanted to reach over and grab the phone from him and just tell the person at the other end to send the item and don't ask any questions. From years of dealing with police procedures I knew that wasn't going to work. It was always an exasperation point for me.

"Fine," I said and dropped my forehead in disgust onto my arm which was lying on the edge of his desk. "I was so close," I muttered. "So close."

The police station din rose and I lifted my head to look around. *Why the sudden buzz?*

"I'll be right back," Williamson mumbled, stood and wandered over to a group of officers.

He stood there listening, nodding his head. The group started to break up and I watched as Williamson ambled back to the desk, pick up his phone and pretend to punch in numbers.

"Turn so your back is to the others and they can't see you talking," he said into the phone. "I'm going to let you in on the low-down."

I squirmed around in my seat until I was leaning against the desk, elbow up and I was resting my cheek in the palm of my raised hand. There was no way anyone could see if my mouth was moving.

"What's up?"

"You were there, right? Yesterday, at E-MIT-C?"

"Yes."

Willie's eyes flared with excitement. "Did you see the lab? Harbinger's secret lab?"

"Sort of," I mumbled. "I didn't get inside it, but saw some of it from the hallway."

"Did you see the eternal machine?"

"The what?" I knew my voice was too loud and I quickly pretended to stretch with a yawn with a loud drawn out 'uh-ya' to cover my act.

Williamson's face was a mixture of ticked and smirk. He was upset I'd let my voice rise, yet trying not to smile at my comic actions. He quickly bent down and spoke into the phone.

"Supposedly Harbinger's machine was able to take a person's blood, purge it of all crap in it and make a person better, even younger. They're saying he could take the blood of a young person, clean it, and put it into an old person and make them younger."

"You mean like a fountain of youth? How?" I wanted to lean in closer but knew I couldn't.

"Did you see the body?"

I didn't need to reply, my wide-eyed stare told Willie I was surprised and knew nothing about it. I moved to the edge of my chair. *Screw it*, my mind screamed and I leaned in. "What body?"

My buddy leaned back in his chair, laughed, and smiled. "Looks like it was probably a run-away, maybe seventeen years old, male and drained of blood."

"Could it have been a cadaver?"

Willie shook his head. "Nope. Seems Harbinger has been playing god. His bank account is pushing seven digits and he doesn't make that kind of money."

"Get his reader. Now!" My voice was hoarse and the words were spoken harshly. "I'll be back." I stood and took two steps from his desk. "When you get finished on the phone, call me." I waved and headed out the door. I was damned sure nobody in the precinct's room suspected anything although Preston watched me leave.

#

I sat at my desk going over my notes. The phone rang.

"I told you to be careful, Mr. Hargrove. Now you have to pay the consequences for—

"Marvin!" CLICK.

Again that little boy and unknown woman assaulted my mental acuity as I worked. *Who were they?*

I checked the phone log — it was Marvin Lashlin's home. Suddenly a chill raced through my body as I remembered the person who stood at the window as I walked by the apartment building. The person was non-moving, staring and although I hated to use a non-technical term, just plain creepy.

The phone rang again. I glanced at the caller id. It was Landelli.

"Hargrove here," I said picking up the phone.

"Were you able to retrieve my reader from Qiang yesterday?"

"I had a long talk with Ren and that one wasn't yours. Seems Qiang has had it longer than—"

The bells went off in my head. *Whose reader was I searching for? Lashlin's? Landelli's?*

There was continued silence at the other end.

"I'm checking into another possibility," I finally said.

"If you mean the one that Harbinger was clinging onto for dear life, forget that. Seems the whole thing had been wiped clear."

"Did you check to see if it was yours?" I asked.

Again I was met with silence.

"Do your job, Detective Hargrove." He hung up.

Do my job, I thought. My mind raced over the facts, or at least what facts I knew, furiously writing them on the sheet of paper in front of me.

The front door opened and I glanced up to see Marvin's sister, Georgiana Lashlin Morrison stomp in, her heels clicking loudly on the floor.

"Do you know where my brother is?"

I shrugged. "In his room?"

"He's not in his room," she snarled. "What have you done with him?"

Jerking back into my chair, I glared at the woman accusing me. It was my turn to get nasty.

"Why don't you ask the resident manager you have on payroll. Wasn't that *his* job — to baby sit your brother?"

Mrs. Morrison sat in the chair before the desk and broke down into tears. "He opened the apartment for me when Marvin wouldn't answer the door."

"You mean he didn't tell you to go away?"

Her brows knitted together in a frown and she slightly shook her head. "Whatever do you mean? I tapped gently on the door and begged for him to let me in." She held her hankie to her nose. "Marvin just ignored me, so I finally offered the manager fifty dollars to let me in." She sat up straight in the chair and blinked her eyes to rid them of any tears. "He used his pass key." She paused. "Marvin wasn't in there. I've waited all morning."

"Fine," I said. "Let's go back to the apartment. Maybe I'll find something to tell me where he's gone. I tried to talk to him yesterday and he wouldn't let me in, he just kept yelling at me to leave him alone and go away."

CHAPTER EIGHT

"It's a simple thing, Russ," I said while slapping him on the back like an old friend. "Either you let us into her brother's apartment, no money, or I tell your boss about the money-making scam you've got going on." I batted my eyes innocently at him like a two-bit hooker. He knew he was had and I wasn't about to the pay extortion money.

"Fine," he snarled, put the beer on the table, grabbed a set of keys and stomped up the stairs and to the end of hallway. He rapped on the door and inserted the key.

"Leave me alone," Marvin said from the other side.

Russ stepped back, yanking his keys with him, his eyes as wide open in shock as possible. "Honest to God, I never saw him come in."

"He ain't in," I said. "That has to be a recording." I knocked on the door.

"Go away. Leave me alone."

I knocked again.

"Leave me alone. Go away. I'm busy."

I knocked yet again.

"Leave me alone."

"Whatever are you doing, Detective Hargrove?" Georgiana asked.

I winked at her and again knocked on the door.

"Go away. Leave me alone."

Once more I knocked.

"Leave me alone. Go away. I'm busy."

I held up my index finger. "The next time I knock he will say 'leave me alone' – any takers? Fifty bucks, Russ?" I rapped on the.

"Leave me alone."

Russ shoved the key into the door, unlocked it, and snapped the door open for us to enter.

The door banged open and started to come back again, I grabbed it, and knocked.

49

"Go away. Leave me alone."

There, neatly tucked away beside a hanging basket of artificial flowers was the speaker. I spotted the recorder apparatus around the corner on a shelf.

"Why would he have something like that?" Georgiana asked.

"I got a cold beer downstairs getting warm. Lock up when you leave." Russ grabbed the door and shut it behind him as he left.

I ambled over to the machine. With a little research I was able to discern it not only responded to the front door but also answered in-coming calls and could make out-going calls. I pressed buttons and saw where a call had come in and then a call had been made to my office within the last hour.

Exactly what kind of a game was Marvin Lashlin playing?

I glanced up from the machine, my eyes absently looking into the next room off the living room. My natural reflexes kicked in and I jumped back, startled. A person stood at the window. I took a deep breath and approached the room. The stranger never moved.

"Hello?" I called. "Who are you? We thought the apartment was empty."

"Who are you talking to, detective?" Georgiana tip-toed over to me and looked around the open door into the room with me. She stepped back, surprised.

"It appears to be a statue," I replied and flicked the overhead light on.

The room was a complete mess. Files lay on the floor in complete disarray as if somebody in a temper tantrum had tossed a stack into the air. Two cabinet drawers were open and empty. A couch was against the opposite wall with two pillows missing. They were on the floor nearby. The desk which occupied the center of the room was empty of any embellishments as if somebody had swiped their arm across its surface.

"What happened in here?" Georgiana asked. "It looks like this room was ransacked."

My attention was on the statue, the mannequin standing at the window. The curtains had been carefully placed to make it appear she was looking out. This was the person I had seen yesterday peering down at me. I smiled at the memory of it being creepy. *The unknown is always mysterious,* I thought.

"Offhand I'd say either it was ransacked or somebody got extremely upset." I scanned the room one more time. "Definitely appears to be a temper tantrum."

"How can you tell?" Georgiana asked.

"Simple," I replied. "If somebody is looking for something, they can make a mess, toss things around but there remains a certain neatness like files or papers on the desk. If the searcher is your typical television thief, they tear file drawers out, rip couch pillows, and in general, destroy things. If you look, the desk has been cleaned off as if a person got mad and just tossed it all to the floor using their arms to move it away. Some of the papers are scrunched up, again, an indication of anger. Notice the trashcan? It still has items in it. A person searching for something would have emptied it." I nodded my head approvingly at my appraisal. "Definitely a temper tantrum." I glanced over at Mrs. Morrison. "Is your brother prone to these?"

"When he was younger," she mumbled. "He'd get mad at himself and —" Her eyes widened. "This is exactly how his room looked after one of them."

The front door slammed shut.

"Who's here?"

We stepped to the room's door and stared at the short man dressed in a professional dark suit standing in the small foyer. I glanced at my watch, noticing the time: 5:28 p.m. I frowned, not realizing how much time had passed.

"I'm sorry, Marvin," Georgiana said. "When nobody answered the door, I became upset. Where did you go that you got all dressed up?"

"Dr. Landelli," I started, still a little muddled. "Perhaps you can—"

"Landelli?" Georgiana cut me off and stared at me as if I had just spewed a sailor's curse in the midst of a Victorian tea gathering. She pointed at the man before us. "This is my brother, Marvin Lashlin. He lives here."

51

I pointed at the same man. "That is Dr. Landelli who works at E-MIT-C."

The man in question glanced back and forth between us then his eyes clouded. He frowned, his lips pursed and he finally squinted in my direction.

"I told you to be careful," a little boy's voice said calmly.

As I stood there staring at the man before us, he now stood with his head slightly cocked to the side, holding his hands behind him and scuffing his left foot in a mindless kick.

I glanced over at Mrs. Morrison, her face ashen as she stared with horror at the man before us.

"You shouldn't be here, Mr. Hargrove. It's not safe." The man pointed at me, his little boy voice continuing with threats.

Suddenly his eyes clouded and his face contorted into a frown.

"Marvin! Go to your room and clean it," a woman's voice snarled from his throat.

Dr. Landelli, Marvin Lashlin or Marvin the little boy, depending on who you were talking with, jutted out his lower lip in a pout, hung his head and proceeded to shuffle toward the room we had just left moments earlier.

"My God!" I exclaimed. "I've never seen anything like this before."

The man gazed up at me, his eyes re-focusing. "Detective Hargrove! How good of you to visit." It was Dr. Landelli. He stood directly in front of me, grabbing my hand to shake.

"Marvin Lashlin?" Georgiana called softly.

I watched his eyes cloud yet again, a small frown on his face as he slowly recognized me, then turned to face the woman.

"Hi, sis." He glanced nonchalantly about the room, obviously looking for another person. "Sorry, I didn't see you. What are you doing here?" The man walked over to Mrs. Morrison and kissed her on the cheek. "Where's Henry? Have you met Detective Hargrove?" He pointed back at me. "He's here to help me find my stolen reader." The man glanced back in my direction, his face a beacon of hope. "Isn't that correct?"

Suddenly things made sense to me. Lashlin was Landelli and the little boy I'd heard on the phone was him, too, as was the woman. My mind raced and then I remembered another voice, the one which had called me with threats. Was this another personality? Could there be five people inside this one body?

Again Marvin's eyes changed their appearance.

"I have to go clean my room," he whispered in a little boy's voice. "I was bad yesterday and made a mess."

Once more he headed for the room we'd just come out of. Georgiana reached out to touch his shoulder and I quickly grabbed her hand and held her back. I placed an index finger to my lips and nodded back at the couch in the living room. Marvin walked into the room and closed the door behind him, leaving us.

We sat on the couch and I held her one hand as she wept. She wiped her eyes with a hanky she had in her other hand.

"I take it you're not aware of this," I whispered and gazed at the closed doors.

"No," she snapped, her eyes wide in surprise. "Never." She paused and hung her head. "And that woman's voice," she whispered. "It sounded exactly like our mother." She shivered.

I smiled. "To think I was going to ask if Marvin had been adopted." I patted her hand. "I could see a resemblance between your brother and Landelli and started to think perhaps they were twins who were separated at birth."

She looked up at me.

"Don't worry, that has been cleared up. Actually, this has cleared up a lot of things except for a few which I will have to figure out." I stood. "Do you feel safe with your brother?"

Her head jerked and she stared at me. "Of course, he's my brother."

The door clicked open and Marvin walked toward us. Which Marvin I didn't know.

"Detective Hargrove," Landelli's voice was clear. "Since my reader has been wiped clean and it seems when the police finish, it will be returned to me, I no longer need your services."

"I was hired by Marvin Lashlin," I replied. "I think he should

53

be the one to terminate the contract."

"Mr. Lashlin will abide with my wishes," Landelli snapped. "Now, if both of you would be so kind, please remove yourselves from this apartment."

"Marvin Lashlin!" Georgiana yelled. "You apologize this instant."

I reared back at her voice. It was reminiscent of the woman's voice I'd heard on the phone and earlier today. As I watched, Landelli's eyes clouded and then cleared.

"I'm sorry, sis," Marvin Lashlin mumbled.

"Perhaps we should leave," I offered and placed an arm around Georgiana's shoulder and eased her toward the door. "I would like to talk to you tomorrow morning, if I could, Mr. Lashlin?"

He stood there momentarily clicking off mental notes. "How about eight, then?"

"Fine," I replied. "I'll be here in the morning, about eight."

"Sure," Marvin Lashlin replied, an innocent smile spreading across his face.

I consoled and steered Georgiana back to my office.

# # #

As we walked into the building, Henry Morrison was waiting impatiently by my office door.

"You said you were coming over to Hargrove's office," he yelled.

"We went to Marvin's apartment," I said and opened the door. "Please come in. We have a lot to discuss."

I flicked on the light and moved to my desk. Henry and Georgiana took chairs opposite me. She immediately broke down and started crying.

"What the hell is going on?" Henry reached over to console his wife.

I leaned back in my chair. On the walk back to the office I'd had some time to process some of what I'd seen and learned.

"It would seem Marvin Lashlin had a breakdown a couple of

months ago," I started.

Henry nodded his head in agreement.

"But before he had the breakdown, it would appear he had other issues which became more prominent at that time."

Again, Georgiana sobbed loudly and Henry once more reached over and consoled his wife while giving me a questioning look.

I nibbled on my thumbnail nervously. "Marvin Lashlin has a case of DID; dissociative identity disorder, more commonly known as multiple personality disorder."

Henry frowned.

"Your brother-in-law, Marvin Lashlin, is not alone inside his mind. From what I could tell there are definitely four distinct personalities in him." I raised my hand and lifted my index. "One is Marvin Lashlin." Another finger came up. "One is Marvin Landelli." Another finger lifted. "One is little boy Marvin." A fourth finger went up. "Another is what appears to be their mother, Mrs. Lashlin."

Henry sat there frowning and shaking his head. "This is nonsense."

"It isn't," I stated. "In fact, there may be a fifth person in there — the one who threatened me and I thought it to be you."

"But Marvin is such a soft, easy going man."

"I— I saw it," Georgiana choked out.

The phone rang. I reached to answer and noticed the number. I hit the speaker button.

"Hargrove Detective Agency," I said.

"I told you to be careful," the little boy's voice said.

Georgiana's fist immediately went to her mouth and muffled her soft, agonizing scream.

"Now look what you've done." There was a pause. "Detective Hargrove?" It was Landelli's voice. I'd recognize the way he said my name in any conversation. "You really need to solve this case. And quickly."

"Marvin! Hang up tha—" CLICK.

Henry sat there, his jaw hanging down, staring at the phone.

"That is what I was facing when I first took this case," I

started. "Things have gotten more complicated as time has passed and today was the culmination." I looked at Georgiana. "We both got the surprise of our lives when we found out Dr. Landelli and your brother-in-law to be the same person." I leaned forward and placed my elbows on the desk. "In fact, we both got to meet all four of the personalities this afternoon."

Henry leaned over and wrapped a comforting arm about his wife's shoulder, placing her head against his chest. "We'll get through this and he'll have the best doctors." He leaned in close. "Let's go home so you can get some rest. I'm sure this has been a strain on you."

CHAPTER NINE

The phone rang.

"Are we still on for tomorrow night?" There was a pause. "If not, my wife is going to personally kill you. She's getting her hair done early in the morning, and has already hired the babysitter."

I snickered at Willie's concern. "Yes, dinner tomorrow night, and my treat." I realized I didn't have a date. My mind raced to think who I could invite on such short notice.

"You're quiet, Barry. Could you ask Sheila?" Williamson suggested. "Vera really likes Sheila. Actually Vera thinks the two of you should get serious."

My mind instantly conjured up beautiful Sheila. She was perfect and that scared me. *Sheila. The goddess on the pedestal, the chef of the kitchen and the* — I smiled at the memory of the last part. "Uh, I haven't heard back from her," I replied, lying to him but knew I'd be calling her as soon as we hung up. *I just hope she isn't dating somebody else, yet.*

"I got that reader you wanted," Willie whispered. "Can you get over here soon?"

"Consider me out the door," I replied snapping back to reality. "Bye."

I slapped the phone down and headed for the door. Ren Nin stepped through the door startling me.

"I need talk you, detective," Ren said. "Qiang kill my uncle."

"Excuse me?" I staggered back at the words. "He killed your uncle?"

" Shì," he replied. "My uncle owner Chang's restaurant."

"I really don't have the time to—" I glanced around the room while I attempted to figure out an answer to my dilemma. "Come with me," I finally said. "You can tell my friend, Williamson, which will make his job a little easier."

"We go where?" Ren asked nervously.

"Down to the police precinct where I used to work. My buddy is working on Chang's murder."

"Not murder. Accident."

"Fine. You can call it an accident," I said and pushed him out the door while flicking the lock. "You can tell me about it on the way."

"This is supposedly Harbinger's reader he was holding onto so tightly," Williamson said while passing the object to me. "Not a whole lot on it. From what I've heard, he was a giddy idiot when they caught him at the lab."

I grabbed the reader and flipped it over. The cover with the vampire Einstein was there and when I peeled it back, I could see Marvin's name engraved. This was what I was looking for. The button pushed quietly and the screen flickered into life.

There wasn't much to see, two games and three books. I frowned, puzzled, then remembered Marvin said he kept his information inside a book.

"Secrets of Egypt," "Vampiric Lore," and "Ancient Doctors" were the titles. I sat there staring at the titles and finally clicked on "Vampiric Lore" since it had to do with blood. I flipped through pages and found nothing. "Ancient Doctors" was my next choice. Again, nothing. It was obvious the book I should have selected was "Secrets of Egypt" and clicked on it. Once more as I reached the end of the pages, I'd found nothing.

"It must have been removed," I muttered and shook my head disgustedly.

"Please," Ren said and reached for the reader. "You look for book, yes?"

He placed the reader on Williamson's desk and his fingers danced over the screen, quickly pushing digital buttons in conjunction with the controller buttons. I couldn't keep up.

"There," he said proudly. "This book?"

I stared at the title: "Metamorphoses by Ovid; Medea, Book Seven."

"Ovid?" I asked. "Why in the hell would he use that book? Are there other books that have been deleted from the reader?"

"Yes, older books. This last book deleted." Ren smiled at his competency.

Williamson leaned back in his chair. "Medea. Wasn't she the snake lady in mythology?"

"That was Medusa," I said. "I'm working back on memory and my Latin classes." I could feel the wrinkles in my forehead as I scrounged my memory banks for the legends. "But I keep thinking that whole Medea affair had a segment about his father being infused with new blood."

"Interesting concept," Williamson quipped.

I opened the book. After flipping about ten pages, the text disappeared, replaced with images and notations of a device. The exact same device I'd seen in Landelli's lab and also Harbinger's. A shiver scuttled down my spine bringing goose bumps to my arms.

Ren nodded his head approvingly. "I find book."

"Have a seat, Ren," I said and plopped myself into a chair next to Williamson's desk. "Now is the time for you to tell Sgt. Williamson what you shared with me on the way over."

Ren nervously sat before he looked up into the officer's eyes.

"I join tong many years ago. Stupid, but Qiang, my cousin, he join tong. Tong is Blue Lotus Society." He gazed at Williamson for any recognition.

My buddy sat there quietly nodding his head. "I know of it, go on."

"Qiang, he talk and talk. He talk in whisper to my uncle. Last week Qiang tell me bring Uncle Chang to him."

Willie reached down, opened a drawer and pulled out a file and gazed at it momentarily. "That would have been Sunday night?"

" Shì.. uh, yes. I take Uncle Chang. He meet Qiang. He take uncle and tell me go away. He say no tell." Ren sat quietly for a few moments. "Last time I see uncle."

"So you think Qiang killed your uncle? For what purpose?"

"Go ahead, Ren." I pressed Ren to be as truthful as possible. "Tell the nice officer what your uncle said as you went to meet Qiang."

"Uncle Chang member, control tong many years. He say tong make him live forever now. I find out uncle is dead. I no kill him."

"Wait a minute. You're telling me Chang was a member of the Blue Lotus Society tong? What is this crap about him living forever?"

"He call it yǒnghéng de xuè." Ren paused. "It mean eternal blood."

"What?" Williamson yelped.

"Tong want machine. Qiang give tong the new hematological mistifier.

Williamson leaned back and scratched his forehead then pointed at Ren and glared at me. "What the hell is he talking about?"

"As best I can figure out, Marvin Lashlin designed a machine which cleanses the blood and alludes to the possibility of being younger. Marvin Landelli built the machine and Qiang stole one of the more vital elements of the machine to give to the Blue Lotus Society tong." I glanced over at Ren. "So far, right?"

Ren nodded his head in agreement. "My Uncle Chang, he old man. He want be young and control tong forever. Qiang give him the machine."

"You mean that crap they were talking about Dr. Harbinger was all true? Including the blood transfusions?"

"Afraid so, buddy." I grimaced and shrugged. "It would appear something went horribly wrong when they attempted to do this with Chang. They dumped the bodies, both Chang and the young man who obviously hadn't planned on donating his blood."

Williamson leaned in. "Ren, you said Chang was running the tong. Is that correct?"

Ren slowly nodded his head in agreement.

"Who would be in charge of the local Blue Lotus Society tong with Chang out of the way?"

"Tong is family. Bingwen is Chang's eldest son," I offered and then looked at Ren.

He sat there shaking his head. "Bingwen no want tong. He not strong. Weak."

"So somebody else is in now in charge of the tong, but who?" Williamson scanned down the document on Chang.

"Not Qiang," Ren said and snickered. "He no like her."

"Chang's wife? I didn't know he even had a wife." I gasped at the thought of her killing her husband, even accidentally.

"My aunt die many years ago," Ren said quietly. "He have young friend." I watched as he grinned. "That why he want be young."

"A girl friend? Chang had a girl friend? That's why he wanted to be young?" Williamson sat there tapping a pencil on the desk. "I thought you said he wanted to control the tong."

"He impress her. He strong leader."

"Do you know her name?" I asked.

Ren shook his head, his long dark hair rustling in the action. "She work at restaurant."

"Well, that definitely is going to be a problem," Williamson quipped. "Chang's is closed for three weeks. Guess I'll wait until after the funeral on Monday."

"I no kill my uncle," Ren stated. "I free?"

Williamson nodded his head. "I don't have anything to arrest you for other than suspicion, and I don't see any reason for you to sit in jail. Qiang, on the other hand, I might want to bring in for questioning."

My phone rang and I glanced at the name. It was Sheila. "Got to take this," I said and snapped the phone open. "Hi, Sheila." I stood and stepped away from the two. "Yes I do realize it is short notice. I'm sorry," I whispered and waited, knowing full well she was going to decline. "I am taking Williamson and his wife out to Portofino's." I waited longer in silence. "You will? I'll pick you up around 6:40 tomorrow night. Will that work?" It was obvious Williamson knew who I was talking to so I gave him a 'thumbs up' sign. "See you tomorrow. Bye" I snapped the phone shut and glided back toward the desk. I knew there was a strut to my walk. I had a date for tomorrow night.

"You are one lucky jerk," Williamson quipped. "Now, the both of you, get out of here." He shooed us away from the desk. "Ren, you stay close and don't leave town." He turned to me. "Barry, see you tomorrow night and remember, it is all your treat."

CHAPTER TEN

To say I was nervous would have been understatement. Here it was, Friday night and I now stood before the door to Sheila's apartment. I knocked.

"One minute," she shouted and suddenly the door was open and she stood there. "I hope I didn't overdress."

I stood there, wordless. She was a vision in the white form fitting dress accenting every curve. Her dark hair framed her face, ice-blue eyes highlighted in smoky eye shadow, and a fantastic tan had me holding my breath in fear she would disappear.

"Perfect," I finally whispered. "Ready?"

"Almost," she replied. "Help me with the bracelet you gave me?" She handed me the tennis bracelet of rainbow colored sapphires I'd given her for Christmas. "Do you remember it?"

I silently nodded and snapped the clasp together trying to remember why we'd drifted apart. I couldn't remember, and seeing her now, I realized what a mistake it had been.

"I can't believe you're springing for Portofino's Restaurant. Is there a special reason?"

"I promised Williamson I'd treat him and his wife to dinner for helping me," I replied. "Plus the current job is paying well."

She wrapped her arm in mine and we walked out of her apartment into the hallway. In the distance I heard Chinese and a voice I recognized.

"Mei Lin?" I questioned.

"Ah, Mr. Hargrove, so good to see you." She turned to the man with her and pushed him down the hallway away from us.

"I didn't realize you lived here," I said nonchalantly. "Imagine my surprise. Oh, may I introduce my date... well, actually she is your neighbor." The amenities were quickly out of the way and I asked what she planned to do while the restaurant was closed.

"I sit here, read. I go to restaurant and clean. It closed but still get dirty." She giggled and bent her head down to hide her face.

"Enjoy your evening," I offered. "Sgt. Williamson is probably wondering where we are." I eased Sheila away and we sauntered down the hallway to the elevator.

The elevator doors opened and my phone rang. I glanced at the number, recognized it as Willie and flipped it open. "We're on our way, just a small delay. See you in about fifteen minutes."

"Tell me you made reservations," Williamson screamed into the phone at me.

"Yes," I replied snidely. "Try using Marvin Lashlin since he is paying for the meal." I could hear Williamson muttering as I snapped the phone closed.

Twenty minutes later had the four of us sitting at a lovely table with an absolutely gorgeous view of the city and river. The whole evening there was a niggling at the back of my head — something wasn't right. Still, the meal was delicious and the company delightful. I enjoyed listening to Sheila laugh and chat comfortably with Willie's wife, Vera.

"We still haven't been able to locate Qiang," Williamson whispered. "We probably shouldn't talk shop, but I don't know who the idiot was to release him when we booked him with Harbinger. Of course, that's water long gone from this bridge."

"Qiang?" My mind played with the image of the man with Mei Lin earlier. *It could have been Qiang,* I thought. "I might have seen him tonight in Sheila's apartment building. Did you know Mei Lin lives there?"

Williamson's left eye brow cocked up in a questioning glance. "Really? I didn't realize being a waitress at Chang's paid that well."

Sheila reached over and placed her hand over mine. "Are you boys talking shop?" She smiled at me and I wanted to get lost in those ice-blue eyes.

"Not too much," I whispered. "Just wondering how Mei Lin can afford her apartment."

"Actually, she probably pays more than I do since she has a two bedroom with a balcony patio." Sheila furrowed her brows in thought. "I'd say it was something like an extra four hundred more." She smiled and gently shook her head. "Too rich for my blood."

"Maybe she has a roommate," Vera offered. "Didn't you say

there was a young man?"

At the suggestion, my mind immediately went into hyper-drive and another option which I really didn't want to consider popped up. I glanced across the table at my buddy.

"Management would have a fit if what I'm thinking what you two are thinking," Sheila murmured.

Williamson shrugged. "It could happen — waitress by day, courtesan by night."

Vera slapped him on the arm. "Now hush. I'm sure she isn't that type of girl."

"Besides, it is only a two bedroom apartment," Sheila added.

"Maybe she is a den mother," I offered. "Starting small with only two girls."

"Really, Barry, I haven't noticed that much traffic in the hallway to warrant an idea that risqué, whatsoever. Perhaps this young lady has other money."

"Or possibly a male friend who stays over and shares the expenses," Vera added and smiled at her addition to the conversation. "We've talked enough work tonight, especially you two." She pointed at her husband and me. "So, anyone up for a movie? It is too early to go home... and the kids."

"Oh, that sounds wonderful," Sheila gushed. "But, I really need to call it an early night. I have a lot to do tomorrow." She gazed up at me, her eyes taking me away to lands I wanted to visit. "Is that terrible of me?"

I pulled her close and kissed her forehead. "No, that's fine. We can take a rain check on it." The ladies started to say their goodbyes. "See you Monday morning." I reached over and shook Willie's hand, covertly passing him a two fifty dollar bills to pay the babysitter. "That should take care of the babysitter... and a movie for just the two of you," I said softly and smiled at him.

As I held the car door open for Sheila, I had to ask. "You have a busy day tomorrow?"

"Not really," she purred. "Oh, I do have a few things to do, but—"

I rushed around to the other side of the car and slid in. She leaned over and put her head on my shoulder as I started the car.

"I thought," she started, and placed a hand on my shoulder. "It would be nice for just the two of us to spend some time together. I have a bottle of white wine chilling at the apartment."

I knew where this was going and had no objections. I put the car into gear and headed toward her place. The evening was still young and one of the most beautiful women in the world now rested against me.

The apartment building loomed ahead and I started to search for a place to park.

"Here," she said and snapped a security card into view. "Use the basement parking. No reason to leave your car outside all night." She smiled at me, wrapped her arms gently around my arm and once more leaned her head against my shoulder.

Suddenly, all the worries, all the problems of my life were gone. I was relaxed and my mind wandered at the thought of having a family like Williamson did. Perhaps being a bachelor wasn't what I wanted for my life. I parked the car and Sheila quickly jumped out and joined me as we headed for the elevators. I was feeling very good right now and wondered exactly how I'd feel in the morning. *With the woman of my dreams in my arms, how could I feel anything but absolutely wonderful?* I leaned in and gently cupped her chin with my hand, lifted her face and our lips melded in a lingering kiss. This elevator was our world, ours alone.

The elevator doors opened and I could hear two people struggling.

"No, Qiang!"

It was Mei Lin. Qiang was fighting to take something away from her and she fought to hold it. I watched as her leg lifted into the air and struck the side of his head with her foot. *Don't want to meet her in a dark alley fight*, I thought.

"Qiang!" I shouted.

He released the object and stepped away while reaching to his waist. Suddenly he was wielding a gun, aiming it in my direction. He shot. I sidestepped and heard the bullet whiz by me. I lurched forward and grabbed him. He punched me in the gut and I felt the full impact of his youth strike me, bending me over and to my knees. The feeble hold I had on him released and he slipped away. I staggered to my feet and followed him down the hallway toward the stairs.

The door had barely closed as I slammed into it and stopped abruptly to listen on the landing. I leaned over the railing to gaze down the stairs and heard him above me. My feet didn't wait but charged upward, following the small man as he escaped. As I raced up to the highest landing, I heard a door click shut. Two doors. My hand immediately went to the rooftop door. It was locked. I shook my head, either he had locked it or he had indeed entered back into the apartment complex through the other door. I snapped the other door open to see him stepping into the elevator. I rushed over and caught the doors with my hands and was about to pull them back open when I saw him raise the gun and level it with my chest. I lunged to the left and heard the bullet hit the wall behind me. The doors closed.

There wasn't a moment to lose. I raced back to the stairwell and started down to the first floor to face him.

Running and jumping down the stairs for eight floors became a test of stamina. I yanked open the door on the first floor. The elevator doors opened and it was empty. I stared at the empty space and wondered which floor he'd escaped on, which stairwell he would use. Qiang had beaten me.

I leaned against the wall and caught my breath before heading back upstairs. I heard the police car sirens as they approached.

This wasn't in my plans... our plans, I thought as I stood there sweating. *Sheila is going to be pissed. I must smell like a pig now. I* wiped the sweat from my forehead and grinned at a plan. *Maybe she'll join me in the shower?*

I stepped into the elevator and headed back up to her floor and to find out what the hell was going on with Mei Lin.

The elevator doors opened and my knees buckled. Sprawled on the floor, Sheila lay there, blood staining the beautiful white gown. Mei Lin was on her knees beside Sheila, crying. She looked up at me.

"So sorry, Mr. Hargrove." Mei Lin raised her hands to cover her face and she cried even louder.

A group of floor residents stood around, slowly shaking their heads. An elderly man came up and placed a comforting arm over my shoulder. "She'll be missed. Sheila was a wonderful person."

I knelt down and grasped her delicate hand in mine. I wanted to scoop her up and take her to the apartment, place her on the couch and see her eyes flutter open. We'd hug and quickly forget the horror of the night. *That only happens in movies*, I thought.

The second elevator dinged and doors opened. The police stepped out and took control of the situation.

I sat back and leaned against the wall, my body numb. The neighbors disappeared. Mei Lin gave her story. I gave mine. An APB for Qiang was put out.

My phone rang. It was Williamson. I opened the phone and pushed the answer button.

"She's gone," I muttered.

"What the hell happened?"

"Tomorrow, buddy," I replied and snapped the phone shut.

CHAPTER ELEVEN

The night was not the night I'd envisioned. It was one of tossing and turning, of sitting on the edge of the bed, and of crying. It was a night of pacing, and drinking. The sun finally crept through the slightly parted room-darkening curtains and I watched the slowly moving beam of light creep across the floor.

The phone rang. I ignored it and placed my hands over my ears in an attempt to keep my aching head from being attacked any louder.

Coffee, my brain screamed. I stumbled to the kitchen, my head swirling. I started the pot.

I heard somebody at the door. The lock clicked and Williamson strolled into the room.

"Didn't figure you'd answer the door," he said, putting the spare key back in his pocket.

"No reason to answer the door," I replied and offered him my best "give-a-shit" glare through bleary eyes. "Sheila is gone." I heaved a sigh. "Last night, after we left the restaurant, there was no doubt in my mind. She was the one. I was ready to commit to a life with her." Once more I glanced in his direction. "I wanted what you have. I wanted a family. Sheila was the answer."

"They nabbed Qiang early this morning. He was trying for a flight to China." Willie shook his head.

I turned and faced Willie, suddenly feeling very sober. "They got him?"

"Yup, and he's screaming he was set up." Willie ambled over to the coffee pot and poured two cups of black coffee. He grabbed the aspirins and pulled a bottle of water from the frig. "Take these and then I'll give you the coffee."

Three aspirins washed down with icy water followed by gulps of hot coffee. My throat screamed in silent agony.

"I've been a busy boy this morning," Willie said and eased himself into a chair at the table. "Join me." He motioned me to the chair.

I shuffled over to the table and sat, noticed the box of cereal on the counter, reached over and grabbed the box and ate some of the sweetened crap straight out of the box with my hand. "Want some?" I nodded at the box as I placed it on the table.

"No, but I figure you're going to be up and moving here very shortly. We've definitely connected Qiang to Sheila's death, but that was a given." He paused and watched me. "Remember last night when we were joking about how Mei Lin could afford the apartment?"

I inhaled deeply, slouched back in the chair and nodded my head. "Yeah, what of it?"

"That's not her apartment. It is leased by none other than a Mr. Chang." He kept his eyes on me.

"So?"

He smirked. "Buddy boy, this is the same Mr. Chang who is now dead and was the proprietor of Chang's restaurant."

I frowned. My mind refused to concentrate and the billowing clouds of fog wouldn't clear.

"Chang lived there?" It seemed the obvious answer.

"Nope." Willie sat, waiting, allowing a smile to show. "He rented it for a Miss Luli Yu." He paused again and waited for a response. None came, so he nodded his head. "In case you're wondering, this is the same Luli who worked with Mei Lin at Chang's. Also, this is the same Luli who is currently dead."

"Seems Mei Lin has some explaining to do," I said and sipped the coffee carefully.

"It gets better," Willie said with a grin so large it would shame the Cheshire cat. "Seems Mei Lin has a younger brother." He waited for a response from me, none came. "I think you know him." He paused again for dramatic effect.

I shrugged, what did I care?

"His name is Bingwen." Willie waited.

I sat up in my chair. "Bingwen Chang?"

"That's the one," Willie snapped.

My mind cleared faster than parting curtains on opening night for a stage production. "Old man Chang is Mei Lin's father?"

"I see the drugs are finally kicking in to clear your head, Barry," Willie said. "Aspirin and caffeine always make a wonderful combination. Now get dressed since I know you will want to go with me over to Mei Lin's place to ask a few questions."

"Exactly where does Luli come into the picture?" I asked as I tromped back to the bedroom to get dressed. "I'm getting a bad feeling about this."

"I think we'll let Mei Lin explain all the details," Willie replied. "I know you have a lot on your mind right now, but I'm amazed you didn't pick up on some of the details."

"I can't believe I left Sheila there to die while I chased Qiang around the apartment building." Sticking my shirt into my pants, I motioned for Williamson to head to the door. "Let's go, buddy."

I wasn't too thrilled to be heading back to the scene of Sheila's death, but there was a lot at stake here. My mind began to correlate the information.

1) Chang wanted to be young
2) Chang wanted control of tong
3) Chang is dead
4) Luli is dead
5) Qiang and Mei Lin fight
6) Qiang part of tong
7) Chang rents apartment in his name
8) Apartment is for Luli
9) Mei Lin in the apartment

No matter how I tried to work the combination, the result always came up looking bad for both Qiang and Mei Lin. I had a problem with that. I liked Mei Lin. She seemed a good kid and always had been nice to me at the restaurant.

Suddenly, two items blasted to the surface and I blinked at what I hadn't realized. The Blue Lotus Society was a tong and a tong was ruled by a strong person and usually by one family. If Chang had been in control of the tong and lost the position, obviously, one of the family members had taken the position. The question was who? Bingwen didn't strike me as the type to control a tong — he was a business man. Even Ren said Bingwen was weak. Now that I knew

70

Mei Lin was Chang's daughter, the prospect of her running the tong sent a chill down my spine. I remembered the move she used against Qiang last night.

Williamson's phone rang breaking into my thoughts. He spoke quietly and cryptically.

"Nice twist to things," he said putting the phone down. "Seems Dr. Harbinger has never used the machine they found in his lab."

It didn't make sense to me and was about to ask a question when Willie continued.

"Seems the blood they found came from experiments, but none he had performed. He passed a lie-detector test." Willie paused. "Actually, Dr. Harbinger passed the stupid lie detector test four separate times! After some research they discovered our guy, Qiang, had been a very busy boy after hours while supposedly working for Dr. Harbinger."

Williamson rolled up to the apartment building and I scowled at it with a lot of remorse about coming. It was a short ride on the elevator and when the doors opened I tried not to look, but my eyes immediately fell to the floor where Sheila had been last night. The carpet was clean, there were no marks, nothing to indicate last night had even happened other than strong smelling cleaning agents. I looked at her apartment, my chest heavy, and I felt a tear welling up in my eye.

"You okay?"

"Yeah, I'm fine," I snapped and charged toward Mei Lin's apartment. I'd put my best 'tough man' voice into my answer.

"If you'd like to leave—" Willie was apologetic.

"Dammit, I'm here. Let's get the job over with." I rapped on Mei Lin's door.

There was a few seconds pause and then the door shifted open as far as the security chain would allow.

"Oh, Mr. Hargrove. You come?" She smiled at us through the gap.

Sgt. Williamson stepped forward. "We'd like to ask you a few questions. Could we come in?"

" Shì, shì," Mei Lin responded, closed the door and we heard the chain rattle loose. The door opened. "Come in." She motioned to the couch while bowing politely. "Sit, please? I make tea?"

"We won't be needing anything," I said and carefully appraised the apartment taking in the fine leather décor of the furniture, silk curtains, assorted jade and crystal statues. *This ain't the cheap tourist stuff one buys in the markets in Chinatown*, I thought, and picked up a deep green jade egg-shaped carving of a dragon. It appeared as if the artist had intricately fashioned a dragon about an egg and then removed the egg from the center. The jade glowed and the shade of green was amazing.

"A toy my grandfather bring from China when little boy," Mei Lin offered.

I knew enough about jade to know this was Imperial China quality and it pinged like the finest quality European crystal. The glow, the weight — this was no cheap toy and was worth what I was sure to be several thousands of dollars, if not more. Her grandfather might have brought it from China, but it was smuggled in. My search of the room also located an almost translucent white jade smiling Ho Tai Buddha on the elegantly carved side table. *Old man Chang didn't scrimp any coins in decorating*, I thought. *Of course, if he were head of the tong, the spoils would have been quite fine.*

Mei Lin sat opposite us. "You have questions, yes?"

"This is your apartment, do we understand that correctly?" Williamson started.

She nodded her head in agreement.

"Was Luli Yu a roommate then?" Williamson flipped open a notepad. "I noticed her name on the mailbox."

"She live here, but move out. Too expensive."

"Funny," I quipped. "Seems Mr. Chang had leased this apartment, paying a full year."

Mei Lin straightened up in the chair and narrowed her eyes at us. She was thinking.

" Shì. Luli pay Mr. Chang. Now I pay him."

I glanced over at Williamson and he nodded in my direction, giving me free reign to continue the questioning.

"This is really a very nice apartment." I glanced around it again. "Very upscale. Exactly how do you afford this place on your salary as a waitress at Changs?"

"Mr. Chang very nice man. He no charge Luli full price."

"Listen, Mei Lin," I said and leaned nearer to her. "Let's be honest here. You and I both know Chang and Luli were having an affair."

Suddenly the soft, demure little Chinese girl atmosphere was gone. Mei Lin glared at me.

"She too young. He old fool. She take his money." She spat the words from her mouth like a bitter taste.

"Is Qiang your boyfriend?" I asked. It was obvious I had touched on an open wound, and now was the time to spring something she wasn't expecting.

"Qiang think he is. He no strong enough to deserve me."

I reared back in my seat. "What do you mean Qiang is not up to par? Luli is not fit for Chang? Who made you the final judge of all this?"

Mei Lin sat on the edge of her chair, her back straight, hands folded neatly in front of her. "I am Mei Lin. I strong woman."

"Is that why your brother isn't in command of the Blue Lotus Society tong?"

Mei Lin stood. "You go now. No talk." She pointed at the door. "Leave."

"Actually, Mei Lin," Williamson started, "We still have a lot of questions."

"No!" she shouted and stamped her foot.

"Yes," Williamson replied, scolding her like a small child. "Now, sit down. Either you talk to us here, or I will take you down to the precinct."

"I need lawyer?" Mei Lin stood there wringing her hands. "I no answer without lawyer."

"I'm not sure you do, Mei Lin," Williamson said softly. "We're just asking some questions and trying to get a few answers. I haven't accused you of anything. Now, I'm wondering, should I? Do I need to arrest you?"

"No arrest. I talk."

"Fine," I cooed. "Now sit." I patted the arm of the chair she'd been in. "Chang was your father, yes?"

"Shì," Mei Lin answered. "Bingwen my weak brother. He shame family."

"So I am correct in the assumption you are the leader of the tong?"

"Father want tong back. He old. He die. No tong."

I stood and walked over to the side table where Ho Tai still smiled at us. My eyes noticed the small ornate plate with the funny object in it, but I hadn't realized until that very moment what it was. I picked up the 'boggle' and held it between my thumb and index finger. It was then I was sure this was the item that Qiang and Mei Lin had been fighting over last night.

"What is this?" I asked, innocently.

She glanced casually at the item. "Lens." Mei Lin quickly looked out the window.

I held it up and looked out the window with it. "Lens to what?"

Mei Lin sighed loudly. "It lens for telescope." Her voice was agitated. "Why?"

"Isn't this what you and Qiang were fighting over last night when Sheila..." My voice cracked. "When Sheila and I arrived?"

"No. He want that." She pointed at another item beside the statue.

I stared at the palest blue jade flower then picked it up. I was overwhelmed at its beauty and opalescent glow. It was a very rare item, a blue jade lotus blossom. My mind raced to remember what I'd seen her and Qiang fighting over.

"I still think it was this," I said and held up the 'boggle' once more. I held my breath and hesitated before speaking. "This is the hematological mistifier for the bio-amino exchange automaton." The combination of scientific and medical terms flowed from my mouth like a nursery rhyme.

"Say what?" Williamson asked.

"Long story, Willie," I replied. "Dr. Brenner called this—" I held up the lens and smiled. "A boggle on the do-whacker, or in scientific terms, a hematological mistifier for the bio-amino exchange automaton."

"Uh-huh," he mumbled.

"That lens for telescope," Mei Lin whined. "You no believe me?"

"You have a telescope?" I asked and motioned for her to get it.

"Broke," she replied with a grin. "Getting fixed."

"I'm not buying that." I wobbled the lens in my fingers. "I've already seen a duplicate of this at the E-MIT-C labs. I'm guessing this is the final version and the tong leadership, that would be you, wants to control it." I put the lens down and once more picked up the blue lotus blossom.

Mei Lin stood, scowling angrily at me with her arms folded in front of her. She narrowed her eyes and glared at Williamson then back to me.

I turned to my buddy. "I have it. You can verify this with Qiang when you get back to the precinct." I lifted my finger to my lips. "Here's how it went down." I strolled about the room, confident in my knowledge. "Qiang stole a working prototype. Chang had a sweet young thing. Also, he wanted to control the tong, but to do that he had to be young. Mei Lin here wasn't about to give up control without a fight. Qiang had the wrong lens and botched the transfusion for Chang. Then Qiang got the right lens and they tried again with Luli and somebody yet to be discovered or she was just coldly drained of her blood to appear like it had been done via the machine. I'm not sure, but I've got a feeling a lot more people were tested and died." I stopped and looked directly at Mei Lin before once more strolling about the apartment. "Now Qiang wants to be in control of the tong, and is willing to contest you for the position. You've gotten rid of both your father and his girlfriend. You can manipulate your brother since he is weak." I turned again to Mei Lin. "You almost pulled this off."

"You may think you have this all figured out, Detective Hargrove, but you are wrong," Mei Lin said in perfect English. A smile crossed her lips. "You have yet to prove anything of me being involved with the bio-amino exchange automaton or —" She pointed at the boggle. "Or that particular item actually being a hematological mistifier."

Williamson's jaw drooped as he stared at the Chinese woman. "You speak excellent English."

"Of course I do." She scowled at Williamson with disdain. "My father made sure I had an excellent education which included a college degree from a well-respected university. His mistake was assuming I would remain a subservient woman, especially a waitress at a Chinese restaurant." She rolled her eyes and grinned. "Customers don't tip somebody who speaks perfect English." She shrugged. "So I spoke pidgin-English to give customers the illusion they wanted, much like Luli Yu pretended to be in love with my father. That whore was after my father's business and money only. She never loved him. My brother is too wrapped up in the business aspects to understand the world about him." Mei Lin took the blue lotus blossom from my hand and gently placed it back on the side table and then placed the lens on the opposite side, away from the blue blossom. "Something with as much power as this..." She touched the blue jade lotus blossom. "It doesn't belong in the hands of a non-believer."

"Is that the Blue Lotus Society totem?" I asked.

Mei Lin glanced at Williamson, ignoring me. "I believe this is where you arrest me, read me my Miranda rights, and take me down to the precinct for further questioning." She held out her hands, waiting for Willie to put the cuffs on. "Oh, wait, before we leave I want to call my attorney." She giggled. "That way I can call anyone else I want when I demand my phone call."

"You seem very confident," I said, carefully picking up the lens once more in my fingers. "This is what I'd call a pretty incriminating piece of evidence."

"It has your fingerprints, not mine," she said. "I do believe you planted that evidence." She reached down and picked up the phone. She held up her index finger to silence us. "Just a minute while I make a call." She dialed. "This is Mei Lin Chang. I need a lawyer immediately at the precinct. Thank you." She hung up. "Let's go, gentlemen. I have a lawyer waiting for me."

Williamson placed the cuffs on, all the while reciting the Miranda rights to Mei Lin.

"Qiang is going down for this," Mei Lin said with a smile. "I will be out within twenty-four hours."

Williamson looked at me as I looked at him. "Nah," he whispered. "She won't." He smiled and nodded toward the lens. "Just don't muddle her fingerprints."

I carefully placed the lens in a plastic evidence bag. "You seemed to have forgotten, you inadvertently moved the lens to the other side of Ho Tai here." I nodded at the statue. "See? He's happy and laughing at you, Mei Lin."

THE END

About The Author

My name is Robert S. Nailor but most people call me Bob.

I'm retired from the federal government. I was a computer geek and still do some programming yet today. One would think I should have plenty of time to write but I actually seem to have less now. So, to make sure that things work out correctly, I try to force myself to sit down and write. That doesn't always work. Today, writing is fun and I find it relaxing. I get to visit those fantastic and strange places within my mind and well, if I don't come back right away, there is no longer somebody behind me writing on a pink sheet of paper.

I live with my wife, Violet, in a ranch home snuggled into a small wooded acre in NW Ohio. I was born in Sioux City, Iowa, but my parents moved to Ohio in 1953. I have four sons and currently have ten grandchildren and five great-grandchildren.

My interests are travel (have RV, will travel), gardening, music, cooking and reading. So where do I travel? I've been in 47 of the 50 states and strangely, Hawaii is one of the states I've visited. I have also visited two of our territories - Puerto Rico and Virgin Islands. Traveling allows me to add the ambiance to my stories and to some of the characters, also. Gardening is a bit gamey since we live in the country and have the wildlife visiting us constantly — deer, rabbits, raccoons, birds, squirrels and many others. So vegetables don't always make it to harvest but what does is more than tasty. There are flowers, sometimes too many, to keep me busy. Music? I love New Age music and my favorite group is Mannheim Steamroller... and not just because of their fabulous Christmas albums. I was hooked on them before that. I also have created some of my own electronic music which I've been told is pretty good. Should I mention cooking? I love to cook and do gourmet cooking. Having worked with Boy Scouts for several years, I have taught many boys the basics of cooking beyond hotdogs and beans. I have won quite a few contests. As to what I read. Well, obviously a lot of science fiction, fantasy and some Christian. Horror, romance, adventure and other genres are also great reads when they catch my attention with an intriguing tag line or cover.

Bibliography

Novels:

The Secret Voice ~ a Christian story about a young Amish man singing during the 60s racial period
Pangaea, Eden Lost ~ a Barclay Havens, relic hunter mis-adventure
Ancient Blood: The Amazon~ a vampire series, 500 years in waiting
Three Steps: The Journeys of Ayrold ~ an Irish fantasy for today
2012 Timeline Apocalypse ~ the Mayan calendar comes to an end

Anthologies:

At Death's Door ~ a collection of horror stories involving death in some manner, not too much gore, more playing with your mind.
52 Weeks of Writing Tips ~ tips to improve one's writing ability
Telling Tales of Terror ~ essays on how to write horror and dark fiction
Mother Goose Is Dead ~ a collection of favorite fairy tales, fractured
Dead Set: A Zombie Anthology ~ a collection of unusual zombie tales
The Complete Guide to Writing Paranormal-Vol 1 ~ various essays
Nights of Blood 2 ~ different takes on the vampire story
Guide to Writing Science Fiction ~ essays on writing science fiction
Firestorm of Dragons ~ an eclectic collection of dragon stories
Fantasy Writer's Companion ~ essays on writing fantasy
13 Night of Blood ~ 13 amazing vampire tales
Spirits of Blue & Gray ~ a collection of Civil War ghost stories

PLUS more information at www.bobnailor.com

Book Two: The Babbling Sphinx

CHAPTER ONE ~ The Mansion

"May I help you?" the gate's squawk box grated into life.

"Detective Barry Hargrove to see Amelia Eggers."

"Do you have an appointment?"

"Not really," I said. "When I spoke with her this morning, she said she'd notify... ah, the name is..." I struggled through my notes. "Uh... yes, Aswad. She was going to notify Aswad of my arrival."

"One minute, please."

I looked at my old Bulova and watched the timepiece click off the seconds. Twenty-two seconds.

"The gates will open Detective Hargrove. Drive the main road to the house and park beside the statue of Osiris with the smaller statue of Anubis at his feet." There was a pause. "You do know who and what Osiris and Anubis are?"

Osiris? Anubis? The thought was a question. *Sure I knew who Osiris and Anubis were; Egyptian gods.* I rolled a shoulder and waited for the large steel gate to glide to one side.

During the quarter-mile drive I noticed the mansion, to the west of the mansion, a large glass structure, and something in a sandstone color. I attempted to glance between the trees and shrubs for a better view. The tree and bush-lined driveway opened and the mansion stood in its full glory. I parked under the blank stare of twenty-foot-tall Osiris, god of birth and death. At his feet, a six-foot statue of Anubis stood guard.

I strolled on the large inlay of stones creating the majestic entryway before the main door of the mansion. The residence reminded me of an Egyptian temple. I took a moment to take in the vista. I frowned. The pond's Oriental decor confused me. A large circular driveway enclosed a huge pool of crystal-clear water. A fountain sprayed upward and a beautiful pagoda stood in the middle of an island within the pool.

I watched it for a moment, seeing the intricate painted tiles glisten in the sunlight.

That can't be gold, I thought. Yet, it didn't appear to be otherwise. I glanced back at the ebony statue of Anubis. *Onyx*, I thought. I shook my head. It had to be since it didn't appear to be a black painted statue. There was no doubt in my mind that Osiris was marble. I inhaled deeply, taking in the scents. *Obviously, no expense was too much*, I thought.

The door glided open as I approached.

"Welcome, Detective Hargrove. My name is Aswad. Mrs. Eggers is in her library. Please, follow me."

Her library? I thought. *Usually it is just the library.* I grinned at the idea. *A his and her library.*

He closed the door behind me, stepped around, and proceeded across the grand foyer with the dual staircases leading to the upper level. A ten-foot-wide crystal chandelier draped from above. A glass dome above allowed for the sunlight to glisten, sparkle and diffuse throughout the foyer. A million rainbows floated everywhere.

The butler opened a set of double doors and motioned for me to enter. I felt a slight breeze as the doors closed behind when I entered the library. The doors clicked shut.

Amelia stood by a desk, her hands holding an open scroll. I surveyed the room. Books, more books, and hundreds of scrolls cluttered the myriad shelves. She had changed into a different outfit. Gone was the morning frock consisting of a silver lamé evening gown with a sparkling rhinestone top. Instead she now wore a simple kalasiris, a simple linen tube dress, cinched at the waist with a jewel encrusted belt.

I ambled to the desk, taking the time for me to purvey the scrolls Amelia had stretched across it.

"Do you read hieroglyphics?" she asked, noticing my glancing at the scrolls.

"I'm familiar with a few of the symbols," I replied and pointed. "This is Ra." I cocked my head. "And this one is Cleopatra VII. Interesting." I smiled. "The last pharaoh of Egypt."

"You amaze me, Detective Hargrove," Amelia moved to glance at the symbols. "You're quite correct."

"Such a pity Cleopatra died at such a young age. Viper's bite." I leaned to open another scroll, one that appeared quite new.

"If you don't mind," Amelia said. "Please don't touch them with your hands." She removed her gloves. "The human oils can damage such artifacts as these."

"My apologies," I offered. "I thought these to be copies. I didn't realize they—" I stopped and leaned in for a closer look. "This is genuine papyrus."

"Yes, Detective Hargrove," Amelia said. "Mr. Eggers allows me several luxuries. I travel to Egypt and send home these artifacts.

I considered her words. Artifacts? Something told me these were stolen goods, rustled from a tomb. I surveyed the room, this time with my interest on the scrolls. My mind staggered at the number of them as I studied the shelves, counting silently as I estimated how many. Over three hundred.

"What do your books contain?" I asked and pointed randomly at different books on the shelves.

"Various subjects," she replied. "Some history. Some art. Some... shall I say, for the most part, the books are esoteric except to the more discerning types. My heritage lives in me. I am one of the few Egyptians who can prove the purity of their lineage."

I nodded. *Impressive*, I thought.

"Now, if you could show me a few things." I took out my notepad. "I would like to see where you last saw your husband." I hesitated. "The balcony as you called it? Also, his bedroom and the sun room. I will want to spend the most time in those locations, but I still wish to see the other rooms and if you don't mind, I will wander the estate grounds."

"This way, detective," Amelia said. "We will go upstairs to see his bedroom, my bedroom, and the other rooms on that floor.

"You mentioned a nurse. I was wondering—"

"She will be sitting in his bedroom. Her name is Susan Williams."

I frowned, unsure why the nurse would be in Mr. Eggers room.

Amelia opened a door. "This is my husband's bedroom."

A young woman dressed in a freshly pressed white uniform stood as I entered.

"May I introduce, Miss Susan Williams, his attending nurse." Amelia turned to me. "This is Detective Hargrove."

I strode over to her, my notepad in hand.

"Glad to meet you, Miss Williams. Now, as I understand, you were the last person to see Mr. Eggers? Is that correct?"

The young woman blanched, stepping back.

"I didn't see Mr. Eggers last night," she mumbled. "I came on shift at eight this morning. According to Miss Rines, he didn't come into the bedroom. It was assumed he was in... I mean, he decided to..." She shook her head. "Miss Rines said she was alone all night."

"And this Miss Rines is who?" I held pen to paper, waiting for the answer.

"There are three nurses, Detective Hargrove," Amelia interrupted. "They work twelve hour shifts with twenty-four hours off." She smiled. "The other two nurses are Janet Rines and Kathy Whittaker."

"Fine," I said and scribbled a note in my pad. "May I have your address and phone, Miss Williams?"

"I live here," she said. "As do the other two nurses."

"So, basically you sit here twelve hours, keeping tabs on Mr. Eggers. Is that correct?"

Susan nodded. "We are here in case of an emergency."

"Emergency," I repeated. "Such as?"

"If the electricity were to go off, Mr. Eggers' c-pap machine would stop working and if he is in a sound sleep, he could possibly suffocate."

I turned to Amelia. "Really? A mansion with no backup generator?"

"It turns on within three seconds of power shortage." Susan was quick to answer.

I smiled. "At least, the suffocation aspect is of no concern."

"We are trained, Detective Hargrove, for any emergency including a heart attack." Susan cocked an eye of attitude. "If the power went out, the lack of air flow to Mr. Eggers c-pap mask might be enough to cause him to go into a cardiac arrest. You do realize that mask is his only source of air."

"I am quite familiar with c-pap machines; my father has one. Now, what would you do if he died of natural causes during the night?" I asked.

She gave me a quizzical look. "Natural causes?"

I shrugged. "Mr. Eggers is a gentleman up in his years. At some point, the heart is going to just plain stop."

"We immediately begin resuscitation efforts." She heaved a sigh. "Our job is to keep Mr. Eggers alive as long as possible."

I wrote in my notepad: eternal life - right.

"We all die, Miss Williams," I finally said. "For now, that's the only questions I have." I paused. "Oh, wait. Was Mr. Eggers on any medications?"

"Yes, he had a few." She reached for a sheet of paper on the bedside table. "Here's a list of them." She handed me the list. "Some for his heart, some for his blood pressure, and a few others."

I scanned the list. Nothing seemed out of place. I recognized most of the medications.

"Thank you, Miss Williams," I said and, once more, surveyed the bedroom with its heavy brocade curtains, dark wood paneling, plush carpeting and expensive art work adorning the walls.

Then it caught my eye. A snapshot of the sphinx near the pyramids of Egypt. It was so out of place with the other paintings by the greats: Rembrandt, van Gogh, Monet, da Vinci, Dali, and Picasso.

I pointed at the photo. "Interesting shot," I said.

"On our honeymoon," Amelia offered. "That is us standing in front of Great Sphinx of Giza. Our guide snapped the shot. Gregory loves Egypt."

I frowned. "I thought you said he was a recluse, never leaving the mansion grounds. This is what? Six years ago?"

"The picture was 'doctored' to put him in the image. I went. He stayed here and we had him dressed like that and he was super-imposed in to create a new picture. We have others throughout the mansion. Gregory loves to travel."

A world traveler who never leaves home, I thought. "Now, if you don't mind, may I see your room?"

Amelia nodded and I followed.

It was exactly as I imagined it. I noted the emergency button on the nightstand she had told me about. Sheer curtains billowed as the wind entered the room through the huge arched door way to a balcony. I could smell cinnamon and... My mind searched for the scent. It lingered just on the edge of my mind.

Licorice! It was an earthy scent and there was more.

I stared out the doorway to the balcony as the curtains once more wafted into the room. In the distance I could see the pyramidal greenhouse. My mind wandered.

Shaking the cobwebs out of my brain, I returned to my inspection of Amelia's bedroom. Shades of lavender, rouge red, pristine yellow mixed with the black lines. Definitely very Egyptian appearing. She did enjoy her heritage.

I nodded. "Guess I should check out the main floor..." I hesitated. "And where the party was held." I once more gazed out the window. "Oh, and I must go walk the grounds." I smiled at Mrs. Eggers. "Of course, first I want to see where you last saw your husband. If I remember correctly, it was a balcony?" I frowned. "On the first floor?"

She nodded and led me down the magnificent staircase. I watched the rainbows dance about the foyer. It was magical and mesmerizing.

"The party was held here." She opened the doors to a large room. "I understand Gregory's parents had grand parties here when they were alive." She shrugged. "I'm told the parties were the social events of the year."

I nodded my head while taking in the sheer size of the room. It could easily hold over one hundred guests with sufficient room to dance and hold tables laden with foodstuffs.

She strode across the open space. "Gregory was here, speaking to the Chinese dignitaries and then they went out over there." She pointed toward the main doors. "I went to this balcony." She sashayed to the double doors. "It is more of an opening to allow fresh air to circulate in than a true balcony." She shrugged. "Still, it allows me to step from the room. I could see and hear some of what was going on."

"Which was all spoken in Chinese, is that correct?" I asked, remembering what she had told me earlier that day when she hired me.

Again, she nodded. "I don't know who the stranger was, but when things became hostile, Gregory's security men assisted the person to the backseat of the limo." She attempted a feeble smile. "The Chinese dignitaries apologized and bowed many times over as the vehicle drove away."

I watched her.

Amelia heaved a heavy sigh. "That was the last time I saw my husband. I went back to the party." She gazed at me, her eyes widening. "I was the hostess. There were guests, after all. I couldn't just disappear." She shrugged. "Plus, the Chinese dignitaries rejoined the festivities, but Gregory wasn't with them. I figured he was either talking with somebody outside, or he'd escaped to his office.

www.ingramcontent.com/pod-product-compliance
Lightning Source LLC
Chambersburg PA
CBHW070530130626
46555CB00003B/1357